Dave Darrin's Fourth Year at Annapolis

H. Irving Hancock

DAVE DARRIN'S FOURTH YEAR AT ANNAPOLIS

Headed for Graduation and the Big Cruise

H. IRVING HANCOCK

CONTENTS

CHAPTERS

CHAPTER I

WANTED—-A DOUGHFACE!

"Now, then, Danny boy, we——-"

First Classman Dave Darrin, midshipman at the United States Naval Academy, did not finish what he was about to say.

While speaking he had closed the door behind him and had stepped into the quarters occupied jointly by himself and by Midshipman Daniel Dalzell, also of the first or upper class.

"Danny boy isn't here. Visiting, probably, " mused Dave Darrin, after having glanced into the alcove bedroom at his right hand.

It was a Saturday night, early in October. The new academic year at the Naval Academy was but a week old. There being no "hop" that night the members of the brigade had their time to spend as they pleased. Some of the young men would need the time sadly to put in at their new studies. Dave, fortunately, did not feel under any necessity to spend his leisure in grinding over text-books.

Dave glanced at his study desk, though he barely saw the pile of text-books neatly piled up there.

"No letters to write tonight, " he thought "I was going to loan Danny boy one of my two new novels. No matter; if he'd rather visit let him do so. "

In the short interval of recreation that had followed the evening meal Dave had missed his home chum and roommate, but had thought nothing of it. Nor was Dave now really disappointed over the present prospect of having an hour or two by himself. He went to a one-shelf book rack high overhead and pulled down one of his two recent novels.

"If I want Danny boy at any time I fancy I have only to step as far as Page's room, " mused Dave, as he seated himself by his desk.

An hour slipped by without interruption. An occasional burst of laughter floated down the corridor. At some distance away, on the same deck of barracks in Bancroft Hall, a midshipman was industriously twanging away on a banjo. Darrin, however, absorbed in his novel, paid no heed to any of the signs of Saturday-night jollity. He was a third of the way through an exciting tale when there came a knock on the door—-a moment later a head was thrust in.

Midshipman Farley's head was thrust inside.

"All alone, Darry? " called Mr. Farley.

"Yes, " Dave answered, laying his novel aside after having thrust an envelope between pages to hold the place. "Come in, Farl. "

"Where's Dalzell? " inquired Farley, after having closed the door behind him.

"Until this moment I thought that he was in your room. "

"I haven't seen him all evening, " Farley responded. "Page and I have been yawning ourselves to death. "

"Danny boy is visiting some other crowd, then, " guessed Darrin. "He will probably be along soon. Did you want to see him about anything in particular? "

"Oh, no. I came here to escape being bored to death by Page, and poor old Pagey has just fled to Wilson's room to escape being bored by me. What are these Saturday evenings for, anyway, when there's no way of spending them agreeably? "

"For a good many of the men, who want to get through, " smiled Dave, "Saturday evening is a heaven-sent chance to do a little more studying against a blue next week. As for Danny boy, I imagine he must have carried his grin up to Wilson's room. Or, maybe, to Jetson's. Danny has plenty of harbors where he's welcome to cast his anchor. "

"May I sit down? " queried Mr. Farley.

"Surely, Furl, and with my heartiest apologies for having been too dull to push a chair toward you. "

"I can easily help myself, " laughed the other midshipman, "since there's only one other chair in the room. "

"What have you and Page been talking about tonight? " asked Dave.

"Why do you want to know? "

"So that I won't run the risk of boring you by talking oh the same subject. "

"Well, " confessed Midshipman Farley, "we've been talking about this season's football. "

"Oh, dear! " sighed Darrin. "That's the only topic really worth talking about. "

"Speaking of football, " resumed Farley, "don't you believe that we have a stronger eleven than we had last year! "

"If we haven't we ought to walk the plank, " retorted Dave. "You remember how the Army walloped us last year? "

"That was because the Army team had Prescott and Holmes on it, " rejoined Farley quickly.

"Well, they'll have 'em this year, too, won't they?

"So Prescott and Holmes are to be out for the Army this year! "

"I haven't heard anything definite on that head, " Dave answered. "But I take it as a matter of course that Prescott and Holmes will play once more with the Army. They're West Point men, and they know their duty. "

"What wonders that pair are! " murmured Farley with reluctant admiration for the star players of the United States Military Academy. "Yet, after all, Darry, I can't for the life of me see where Prescott and Holmes are in any way superior to yourself and Dan Dalzell. "

"Except, " smiled Dave, "that Prescott and Holmes, last year, got by us a good deal oftener than we got by them—-and so the Army lugged off the score from Franklin Field. "

"But you won't let 'em do it this year, Darry! "

"Dan and I will do all we can to stop our oldtime chums, now of the Army, " agreed Dave. "But they're a hard pair to beat. Any one who saw Prescott and Holmes play last year will agree that they're a hard pair of nuts for the Navy to crack. "

"We've got to beat the Army this year, " Farley protested plaintively.

"I certainly hope we shall do so. "

"Darry, what is your candid opinion of Wolgast? "

"As a man? "

"You know better! "

"As a midshipman? "

"Darry, stop your nonsense! You know well enough that I'm asking your opinion of Wolgast as captain of the Navy eleven. "

"He seems inclined to be fair and just to every member of the squad, so what more can you ask of him. "

"But do you think he's any real good, Darry, as captain for the Navy? "

"I do. "

"We ought to have had you for captain of the team, Darry, " insisted Farley.

"So two or three other fellows thought, " admitted Dave. "But I refused to take that post, as you know, and I'm glad I did. "

"Oh, come, now!

"Yes; I'm glad I refused. A captain should be in mid-field. Now, if Dalzell and I are any good at all on the gridiron— —-"

"Oh, Mr. Modesty! "

"If we're of any use at all, " pursued Darrin, "it's only on the flank. Now, where would the Navy be with a captain directing from the right or left flank. "

"Darry, you funker, you could play center as well as Wolgast does. "

"Farl, you're letting your prejudices spoil your eyesight. "

"Oh, I've no prejudice at all against Wolgast, " Farley hastened to rejoin. "Only I don't consider him our strongest man for captain. Now, Wolgast— —-"

"Here! " called a laughing voice. The door had opened, after a knock that Darrin had not noticed.

"Talking about me? " inquired Midshipman Wolgast pleasantly, as he stopped in the middle of the room.

Midshipman Farley was nothing at all on the order of the backbiter. Service in the Brigade of Midshipmen for three years had taught him the virtue of direct truth.

"Yes, Wolly, " admitted Farley without embarrassment. "I was criticizing your selection as captain of the eleven. "

"Nothing worse than that? " laughed First Classman Wolgast.

"I was saying—-no offense, Wolly—-that I didn't consider you the right man to head the Navy eleven. "

Midshipman Wolgast stepped over to Farley, holding out his right hand.

"Shake, Farl! I'm glad to find a man of brains on the eleven. I know well enough that I'm not the right captain. But we couldn't make Darry accept the post. "

Midshipman Wolgast appeared anything but hurt by the direct candor with which he had been treated. He now threw one leg over the corner of the study table, though he inquired:

"Am I interrupting anything private? "

"Not in the least, " Dave assured him.

"Am I intruding in any way? "

"Not a bit of it, " Darrin answered heartily "We're glad to have you here with us. "

"Surely, " nodded Farley.

"Now, then, as to my well known unfitness to command the Navy football team, " continued First Classman Wolgast, "do either of you see any faults in me that can be remedied? "

"I can't, " Dave answered. "I believe, Wolly, that you can lead the team as well as any other man in the squad. On the whole, I believe you can lead a little better than any other man could do. "

"No help from your quarter, then, Darry, " sighed Midshipman Wolgast. "Farl, help me out. Tell me some way in which I can improve my fitness for the post of honor that has been thrust upon me. I assure you I didn't seek it. "

"Wolgast, my objection to you has nothing personal in it, " Farley went on. "With me it is a case simply of believing that Darry could lead us on the gridiron much better than you're likely to. "

"That I know, " retorted Wolgast, with emphasis. "But what on earth are we going to do with a fellow like Darrin? He simply won't allow himself to be made captain. I'd resign this minute, if we could have Darry for our captain. "

"You're going to do all right, Wolgast. I know you are, " Dave rejoined.

"Then what's the trouble? Why don't I suit all hands? " demanded the Navy's football captain.

Darrin was silent for a few moments. The midshipmen visitors waited patiently, knowing that, from this comrade, they could be sure of a wholly candid reply.

"Have you found the answer, Darry? " pressed Wolgast at last.

"Yes, " said Dave slowly; "I think I have. The reason, as I see it, is that there are no decidedly star players on this year's probable eleven. The men are all pretty nearly equal, which doesn't give you a chance to tower head and shoulders above the other players. Usually, in the years that I know anything of, it has been the other way. There have been only two or three star players in the squad, and the captain was usually one of the very best. You're plenty good enough football man, Wolgast, but there are so many other pretty good ones that you don't outshine the others as much as captains of poorer teams have done in other years. "

"By Jupiter! Darry has hit it! " cried Farley, leaping from his seat. "Wolly, you have the luck to command an eleven in which most of the men are nearly, if not quite, as good as the captain. You're not head and shoulders over the rest, and you don't tower—-that's all. Wolly, I apologize for my criticisms. Darry has shown me the truth. "

"Then you look for a big slaughter list for us this year, Darry? " Wolgast asked.

"Yes; unless the other elevens that we're to play improve as much as the Navy is going to do. "

At this moment Page and Jetson rapped and then entered. Ten minutes later there were fully twenty midshipmen in the room, all talking animatedly on the one subject at the United States Naval Academy in October—-football.

So the time sped. Dave lost his chance to read his novel, but he did not mind the loss. It was Jetson who, at last, discovered the time.

"Whew, fellows! " he muttered. "Only ten minutes to taps. "

That sent most of the midshipmen scuttling away. Page and Farley, however, whose quarters were but a few doors away on the same deck, remained.

"Farl, " murmured Darrin, "for the first time tonight I'm feeling a bit worried. "

"Over Danny? "

"The same. "

"What's up? " Page wanted to know.

"Why, he hasn't been around all evening. Surely Dalzell would be coming back by this time, unless— —-"

"Didn't he have leave to visit town? " demanded Midshipman Page.

"Not that I've heard of, " Dave Darrin answered quickly. "Nor do I see how he could have done so. You see, Wednesday he received some demerits, and with them went the loss of privileges for October. "

"Whew! " whistled Page.

"What? " demanded Dave, his alarm increasing.

"Why, not long after supper I saw Danny heading toward the wall on the town side. "

"I have been afraid of that for the last two or three minutes, " exclaimed Dave Darrin, his uneasiness now showing very plainly. "Dan didn't say a word to me about going anywhere, but— —-"

"You think, leave being impossible, Danny has Frenched it over the wall? " demanded Farley.

"That's just what I'm afraid of, " returned Dave.

"But why— —-"

"I don't know any reason. "

"Then— —-"

"Farl", broke in Dave hurriedly, almost fiercely, "has anyone a doughface? "

"Yes. "

"Who has it? "

"I don't know. "

"Find it—-on the jump! "

"But—–-"

"There's no time for 'buts, '" retorted Darrin, pushing Farley toward the door. "Find it! "

"And I—–-" added Page, springing toward the door.

"You'll stay here, " ordered Dave.

Darrin was already headed toward his friend's alcove, where Dalzell's cot lay. Page followed.

"The dummy, " explained Darrin briefly.

Every midshipman at Annapolis, doubtless, is familiar with the dummy. Not so many, probably, are familiar with the doughface, which, at the time this is written, was a new importation.

Swiftly Dave and Page worked. First they turned down the clothing, after having hurriedly made up the cot. Now, from among the garments hanging on the wall nearby the two midshipmen took down the garments that normally lay under others. With these they rigged up a figure not unlike that of a human being. At least, it looked so after the bed clothes had been drawn up in place.

Then, glancing at the time, Dave Darrin waited—-breathless.

Farley hastened into the room without losing time by knocking. Under one arm he bore, half hidden, some roundish object, wrapped in a towel.

Without a word, but with a heart full of gratitude, Dave Darrin snatched out from its wrapping the effigy of a male human head. It was done in wax, with human hair on the head.

Dave Darrin neatly fitted this at the top of the outlines of a figure under the bed clothing.

Under the full light the doughface looked ghostly. In a dimmer light it would do very well.

"Thank you a thousand times, fellows, " trembled Dave Darrin. "Now hustle to your own quarters before the first stroke of taps sounds. "

The two useful visitors were gone like a flash. Ere they had quite closed the door, Dave Darrin was removing his own uniform and hanging up trousers and blouse. Next off came the underclothing and on went pajamas.

Just then taps sounded. Out went the electric light, turned off at the master switch.

Dave Darrin dived under the bed clothes on his own cot and tried to still the beating of his own heart.

Two minutes later a brisk step sounded on the corridor of the "deck. "

Door after door was opened and closed. Then the door to Dave's room swung open, and a discipline officer and a midshipman looked into the room.

"All in? " the midshipman called.

A light snore from Dave Darrin's throat answered. In his left hand the discipline officer carried an electric pocket light. A pressure of a button would supply a beam of electric light that would explore the bed of either midshipman supposed to be in this room.

But the officer saw Midshipman Darrin plainly enough, thanks to beams of light from the corridor. Over in the opposite alcove the discipline officer made out, more vaguely, the lay figure and the doughface intended to represent Midshipman Dan Dalzell.

"Both in. Darrin and Dalzell never give us any trouble, at any rate, " thought the discipline officer to himself, then closed the door, and his footsteps sounded further down the corridor.

"Oh, Danny boy, I wish I had you here right at this minute! " muttered Dave Darrin vengefully. "Maybe I wouldn't whang your head off for the fright that you've given me! I'll wager half of my hairs have turned gray in the last minute! "

However, Midshipman Dan Dalzell was not there, as Darrin knew to his own consternation. Dave did not go to sleep. Well enough he knew that he was on duty indefinitely through the hours until Dan should return. If Midshipman Darrin fell into a doze this night he would be as bad as any sentry falling asleep on any other post.

So Darrin lay there and fidgeted. Twenty times he tried to solve, in his own mind, the riddle of why Dalzell should be away, and where he was. But it was a hopeless puzzle.

"Of course, Danny didn't hint that he was going to French it tonight, " thought Dave bitterly. "Good reason why, too! He knew that, if I got wind of his intention, I'd thrash him sooner than let him take such a chance. Oh, Dan! Dan, you idiot! To take such a fool chance in your last year here, when detection probably means your being dropped from brigade, and your career ended! "

For Dave Darrin knew the way of discipline officers too well to imagine that that one brief inspection of the room was positively all the look-in that would be offered that night. Some discipline officers have a way of looking in often during the night. Being themselves graduates of the Naval Academy, officers are sure to know that the inspection immediately after taps does not always suffice. Midshipmen have been known to be in bed at taps, and visiting in quarters of other midshipmen ten minutes later. True, the electric light in rooms is turned off at taps—-but midshipmen have been known to keep candles hidden, and to be experts in clouding doors and windows so that no ray of light gets through into a corridor after taps.

Just how often discipline officers were accustomed to look in through the night, Dave Darrin did not know from his own knowledge. Usually, at the times of such extra visits, Darrin was too blissfully asleep.

Tonight, however, despite the darkness of the room at present, Dave lay wide awake. No sleep for him before daylight—-perhaps not then—-unless Dan turned up in the meantime.

After an interval that seemed several nights long, the dull old bell of the clock over on academic Hall began tolling. Dave listened and counted. He gave an almost incredulous snort when the total stopped at eleven.

Then another long period of waiting. Darrin did not grow drowsy. On the contrary, he became more wide awake. In fact, he began to imagine that he was becoming possessed of the vision of the cat. Dark as it was in the room, Dave began to feel certain that he could distinguish plainly the ghostly figure of the saving doughface in the alcove opposite.

Twelve o'clock struck. Then more waiting. It was not so very long, this time, however, before there came a faint tapping at the window.

Dave Darrin was out of bed as though he had been shot out. Like a flash he was at the window, peering out. Where, after all, was the cat's vision of which he had thought himself possessed? Some one was outside the window. Dave thought he recognized the Naval uniform, but he could not see a line of the face.

Tap-tap-tap! sounded softly. Dave threw the window up stealthily.

"You, Dan? " he whispered.

"Of course, " came the soft answer. "Stand aside. Let me in—-on the double-quick! "

Dave pushed the window up the balance of the way, then stepped aside. Dan Dalzell landed on his feet in the room, cat-like, from the terrace without. Then Dave, without loss of an instant, closed the window and wheeled about in the darkness.

"Hustle! " commanded Dave.

"What about? "

"Get off your uniform! Get into pajamas. Then I'll——-"

Dave's jaws snapped together resolutely. He did not finish, just then, for he knew that Midshipman Dalzell could be very stubborn at times.

"I'll have a light in a jiffy, " whispered Dan "I brought back a candle with me. "

"You won't use it—-not in here, " retorted Dave. "The dark is light enough for you. Hustle into your pajamas. "

Perhaps Midshipman Dalzell did not make all the speed that his roommate desired, but at last Dan was safely rid of his uniform, underclothing and shoes, and stood arrayed in pajamas.

"Now, I'll hide this doughface over night, " whispered Darrin, going toward Dalzell's bed. "At the same time you get the articles of your equipment out from under your bed clothes and hang them up where they belong. "

"I'll have to light the candle for that, " muttered Dan.

"If you do, I'll blow it out. There's a regulation against running lights in the rooms after taps. "

"Do you worship the little blue-covered volume of regulations, Dave? " Dan demanded with a laugh.

"No; but I don't propose to take any chances in my last year here. I don't intend to lose my commission in the Navy just because I can't control myself. "

Dan sniffed, but he silently got his parts of uniform out from between the sheets and hung up the articles where they belonged, in this going by the sense of feeling.

Then, all in the dark as they were, Midshipman Dave Darrin seized his chum and roommate by the shoulders.

"Danny boy, " he commanded firmly, "come over with an account of yourself! Why this mad prank tonight—-and what was it? "

CHAPTER II

SOME ONE PUSHES THE TUNGSTEN

You don't have to know every blessed thing that I do, do you? " demanded Dan Dalzell, in an almost offended tone.

"No; and I have no right to know anything that you don't tell me willingly. Are you ready to give me any explanation of tonight's foolishness?

"Seeing that you kept awake for me, and were on hand to let me in, I suppose I'll have to, " grumbled Dan.

"Well, then?

"Dave, for the first time tonight, I struck my flag. "

"Struck to whom? "

"Oh—-a girl, of course, " grunted Dan.

"You? A girl? " repeated Dave in amazement.

"Yes; is it any crime for me to get acquainted with a girl, and to call on her at her home? "

"Certainly not. But, Dan, I didn't believe that you ever felt a single flutter of the pulse when girls were around. I thought you were going to grow up into a cheerful, happy old bachelor. "

"So did I, " sighed Dan.

"And now you've gone and met your fate? "

"I'm not so sure about that, " Dalzell retorted moodily.

"Do you mean that you don't stand any real show in front of the pair of bright eyes that have made you strike your colors? "

"I'm afraid I don't. "

"Dan, is the game worth the candle, " argued Darrin.

"You're mightily interested in Belle Meade, aren't you? "

"Yes; but that's different, Danny boy. "

"How is it different, I'd like to know? "

"Well, in the first place, there's no guesswork in my case. Belle and I are engaged, and we feel perfectly sure each of the other. I'm so sure of Belle that I dream about her only in my leisure moments. I don't ever let her face come between myself and the pages of a textbook. I am here at the Naval Academy working for a future that Belle is to share with me when the time comes, and so, in justice to her, I don't let the thought of her get between myself and the duties that will lead to the career she is to share with me. "

"Humph! " commented Midshipman Dalzell.

"Above all, Dan, I've never Frenched it over the wall. I don't take any disciplinary chances that can possibly shut me off from the career that Belle and I have planned. Belle Meade, Danny boy, would be the first to scold me if she knew that I had Frenched it over the wall in order to meet her. "

"Well, Miss Preston doesn't know but what I had regular leave tonight, " Danny replied.

"Miss Preston? " repeated Dave his interest taking a new tack. "I don't believe I know her. "

"I guess you don't, " Dan replied. "She's new in Annapolis. Visiting her uncle and aunt, you know. And her mother's with her. "

"Are your intentions serious in this, Danny? " Darrin went on.

"Blessed if I know, " Dalzell answered candidly. "She's a mighty fine girl, is May Preston. I don't suppose I'll ever be lucky enough to win the regard of such a really fine girl. "

"Then you aren't engaged? "

"Hang it, man! This evening is only the second time that I've met Miss Preston. "

"And you've risked your commission to meet a girl for the second time? " Dave demanded almost unbelievingly.

"I haven't risked it much, " Dan answered. "I'm in safe, now, and ready to face any discipline officer. "

"But wouldn't this matter wait until November, when you're pretty sure to have the privilege of town leave again? " pressed Midshipman Darrin.

"By November a girl like Miss Preston might be married to some one else, " retorted Dan Dalzell.

"It was a fool risk to take, Dan! "

"If you look at it that way. "

"Will you promise me not to take the risk again, Danny boy? "

"No. "

"It's a serious affair, then, so far as you are concerned, " grinned Dave, though in the dark Dan could not see his face. "For your sake, Danny, I hope Miss Preston is as much interested in you as you certainly are in her. "

"Are you going to lecture me? "

"Not tonight, Dan. "

"Then I'm going to get in between sheets. It's chilly here in the room. "

"Duck! " whispered Dave with sudden energy.

Footsteps could be heard coming down the corridor. It was a noise like a discipline officer.

Three doors above that of the room occupied by our midshipman friends were opened, one after the other. Then a hand rested on the knob of the door to Dave and Dan's room. The door was opened, and the rays of a pocket electric light flashed into the room.

Dan lay on one side, an arm thrown out of bed, his breathing regular but a trifle loud. Dave Darrin had again found recourse to a snore.

In an instant the door closed. Any discipline officer ought to be satisfied with what this one had seen.

"Safe! " chuckled Dalzell.

"An awfully close squeak, " whispered Dave across the intervening room.

"What if he had started his rounds ten minutes earlier? "

"He didn't, though, " replied Dan contentedly.

Now another set of footsteps passed hurriedly along the "deck" outside.

"What's that? " questioned a voice sharply. "You say that you saw some one entering a room from the upper end of the terrace? "

"Oh, by George, " groaned Dan Dalzell, now beginning to shiver in earnest. "Some meddling marine sentry has gone and whispered tales. "

"Keep a stiff upper lip, " Dave whispered hoarsely, encouragingly. "If the officer returns don't give yourself away by your shaking. "

"But if he asks me? "

"If you're asked a direct question, " sighed Dave mournfully, "you'll have to give a truthful answer. "

"And take my medicine! "

"Of course. "

That annoying discipline officer was now on his way back, opening doors once more. Moreover, the two very wide-awake midshipmen could hear him asking questions in the rooms further along the "deck."

"He's questioning each man," whispered Dave.

"Of course," nodded Dan gloomily.

"It'll be our turn soon."

"D-D-Dave!"

"What?"

"I--I'm feeling ill--or I'm going to."

"Don't have cold feet, old fellow. Take your dose like a man--if you have to."

"D-Dave, I wonder if I couldn't have a real sickness? Couldn't it be something so you'll have to jump up and help me to hospital? Couldn't I have--a--a fit?"

"A midshipman subject to fits would be ordered before a medical board, and then dropped from the brigade," Dave replied thoughtfully. "No; that wouldn't do."

That meddling discipline officer was getting closer and closer. Dave and Dan could hear him asking questions in each room that he visited. And there are no "white lies" possible to a midshipman. When questioned he must answer truthfully. If the officers over him catch him in a lie they will bring him up before a court-martial, and his dismissal from the service will follow. If the officers don't catch him in a lie, but his brother midshipmen do, they won't report him, but they'll ostracize him and force him to resign. A youngster with the untruthful habit can find no happiness at the Naval Academy.

"He--he's in the next room now," whispered Dan across the few feet of space.

"Yes," returned Dave Darrin despairingly, "and I can't think of a single, blessed way of getting you out of the scrape."

"Woof! " sputtered Midshipman Dan Dalzell, which was a brief way of saying, "Here he comes, now, for our door. "

Then a hand rested on the knob and the door swung open. Lieutenant Adams, U.S. N., entered the room.

"Mr. Darrin, are you awake? " boomed the discipline officer.

Dave stirred in bed, rolled over so that he could see the lieutenant, and then replied:

"Yes, sir. "

"Rise, Mr. Darrin, and come to attention. "

Dave got out of bed, but purposely stumbled in doing so. This might give the impression that he had been actually awakened.

"Mr. Darrin, " demanded Lieutenant Adams, "have you been absent from this room tonight? "

"Yes, sir. "

"After taps was sounded? "

"No, sir. "

"You are fully aware of what you have answered? "

"Yes, sir. "

"Very good. "

That was all. A midshipman's word must be taken, for he is a gentleman—-that is to say, a man of honor.

"Mr. Dalzell! "

Poor Dan stirred uneasily.

"Mr. Dalzell! " This time the Naval officer's voice was sharper.

Dan acted as though he were waking with difficulty. He had no intention, in the face of a direct question, of denying that he had been absent without leave. But he moved thus slowly, hoping desperately that the few seconds of time thus rained would be sufficient to bring to him some inspiration that might save him.

"Mr Dalzell, come to attention! "

Dan stood up, the personification of drowsiness, saluted, then let his right hand fall at his side and stood blinking, bracing for them correct military attitude.

"It's too bad to disturb the boy! " thought Lieutenant Adams. "Surely, this young man hasn't been anywhere but in bed since taps. "

None the less the Naval officer, as a part of his duty, put the question:

"Mr. Dalzell, have you, since taps, been out of this room? Did you return, let us say, by the route of the open window from the terrace? "

Midshipman Dalzell stiffened. He didn't intend to betray his own honor by denying, yet he hated to let out the admission that would damage him so much.

Bang! It was an explosion like a crashing pistol shot, and it sounded from the corridor outside.

There could be no such thing as an assault at arms in guarded Bancroft Hall. The first thought that flashed, excitedly, through Lieutenant Adams's mind was that perhaps the real delinquent guilty of the night's escapade had just shot himself. It was a wild guess, but a pistol shot sometimes starts a wilder guess.

Out into the corridor darted Lieutenant Adams. He did not immediately return to the room, so Dave Darrin, with rare and desperate presence of mind, closed the door.

"Get back into the meadow grass, Danny boy, " Darrin whispered, giving his friend's arm a hard grip. "If the 'loot'nant' comes back, get up fearfully drowsy when he orders you. Gape and look too stupid to apologize! "

Lieutenant Adams, however, had other matters to occupy his attention. There was a genuine puzzle for him in the corridor. Just out, side the door of Midshipmen Farley and Page there lay on the floor tiny glass fragments of what had been an efficient sixty-candle-power tungsten electric bulb. It was one of the lights that illuminated the corridor.

Now one of these tungsten bulbs, when struck smartly, explodes with a report like that of a pistol.

At this hour of the night, however, there were none passing save Naval officers on duty. None other than the lieutenant himself had lately passed in the corridor. How, then, had this electric light bulb been shattered and made to give forth the sound of the explosion?

"It wouldn't go up with a noise like that, " murmured the lieutenant to himself. "These tungsten lights don't explode like that, except when rapped in some way. They don't blow up, when left alone. At least, that is what I have always understood. "

So the puzzle waxed and grew, and Lieutenant Adams found it too big to solve alone.

"At any rate, I've questioned all the young gentlemen about the window episode, and they all deny knowledge of it, " Lieutenant Adams told himself. "So I'll just report that fact to the O. C., and at the same time I'll tell him of the blowing up of this tungsten light. "

Two minutes later Lieutenant Adams stood in the presence of Lieutenant-Commander Henderson, the officer in charge.

"So you questioned all of the midshipmen who might, by any chance, have entered by a window? " asked the O. C.

"Yes, sir. "

"And they all denied it? "

"Yes, sir. "

"Did you see signs of any sort to lead you to believe that any of the midshipmen might have answered in other than the strict truth? " continued the O. C.

"No, sir, " replied Lieutenant Adams, and flushed slightly, as he went on: "Of course, sir, I believe it quite impossible for a midshipman to tell an untruth. "

"The sentiment does you credit, Lieutenant, " smiled the O. C. Then he fell to questioning the younger discipline officer as to the names of the midshipmen whom he had questioned. Finally the O. C. came to the two names in which the reader is most interested.

"Darrin denied having been out after taps? " questioned Lieutenant-Commander Henderson.

"He did, sir. "

"Did Mr. Dalzell also deny having been out of quarters after taps? "

"He did, sir. "

Lieutenant Adams answered unhesitatingly and unblushingly. In fact, Lieutenant Adams would have bitten off the tip of his tongue sooner than have lied intentionally. So firmly convinced had Adams been that Dan was about to make a denial that now, with the incident broken in two by the report of the tungsten bulb, Lieutenant Adams really believed that had so denied. But Dan had not, and had Dave Darrin been called as a witness he would been compelled to testify that Dan did not deny being out.

The explosion of the tungsten bulb was too great a puzzle for either officer to solve. A man was sent with a new bulb, and so that part of the affair became almost at once forgotten.

Dan finally fell into a genuine sleep, and so did Dave Darrin. In the morning Dave sought out Midshipman Farley to inquire to whom the doughface should be returned.

"Give it over to me and I'll take care of it, " Farley replied. "Say, did you hear a tungsten bulb blow up in the night! "

"Did It" echoed Darrin devoutly. Then a sudden suspicion crossed his mind.

"Say, how did that happen, Farl? " demanded Dave.

"If anyone should ask you— —-" began the other midshipman.

"Yes— —-? " pressed Darrin.

"Tell 'em—-that you don't know, " finished Farley tantalizingly, and vanished.

It was not until long after that Darrin found out the explanation of the accident to the tungsten bulb. Farley, during Dan's absence, had been almost as much disturbed as had Dave. So Mr. Farley was wide awake. When he heard Lieutenant Adams receive the message in the corridor Farley began to wonder what he could do. Presently he was made to rise, with Page, stand at attention, and answer the questions of the discipline officer.

Soon after Dave and Dan were called up, Farley, listening with his door ajar half an inch, slipped out and hit the tungsten burner a smart rap just in the nick of time to save Dan Dalzell's Navy uniform to that young man.

CHAPTER III

BAD NEWS FROM WEST POINT

Bump! The ball, hit squarely by the toe of Wolgast's football shoe, soared upward from the twenty-five-yard line. It described an arc, flying neatly over and between the goal-posts at one end of the athletic field.

"That's the third one for you, Wolly, " murmured Jetson. "You're going to be a star kicker! "

"Shall I try out the rest of the squad, sir? " asked Wolgast, turning to Lieutenant-Commander Parker, this year's new coach.

"Try out a dozen or so of the men, " nodded coach, which meant, in effect: "Try out men who are most likely to remain on the Navy team. "

"Jetson! " called Wolgast.

Jet tried, but it took his third effort to make a successful kick.

"You see, Wolly, who is not to be trusted to make the kick in a game, " remarked Jetson with a rueful smile.

"It shows me who may need practice more than some of the others—-that's all, " answered Wolgast kindly.

With that the ball went to Dave. The first kick he missed.

"I can do better than that, if you'll give me the chance, " observed Darrin quietly.

At a nod from Coach Parker, Dave was allowed five more trials, in each one of which he made a fair kick.

"Mr. Darrin is all right. He won't need to practice that very often, Mr. Wolgast, " called coach.

Then Dan had his try. He made one out of three.

"No matter, Danny Grin, " cried Page solacingly, "we love you for other things that you can do better on the field. "

Farley made two out of three. Page, though a rattling good man over on the right flank, missed all three kicks.

"I'm a dub at kicking, " he growled, retiring in much disgust with himself.

Other midshipmen had their try, with varying results.

"Rustlers, forward! " shouted Lieutenant-Commander Parker.

Eleven young fellows who had been waiting with more or less patience now threw aside their blankets or robes and came running across the field, their eyes dancing with keen delight.

"Mr. Wolgast, let the Rustlers start the ball—-and take it away from 'em in snappy fashion! " admonished coach.

The game started. In the second team at Annapolis there were some unusually good players—-half a dozen, at least, who were destined to win a good deal of praise as subs. that year.

Tr-r-r-ill! sounded the whistle, and the ball was in motion.

Yet, try as he did, the captain of the Rustlers made a side kick, driving the ball not far out of Dave Darrin's way. It was coming, now, in Dan's path, but Dalzell muttered in a barely audible undertone:

"You, Davy! "

So Darrin, playing left end on the Navy team, darted in and caught the ball. He did not even glance sideways to learn where Dan was. He knew that Dalzell would be either at his back or right elbow as occasion demanded.

"Take it away from Darry! " called Pierson, captain of the Rustlers. "Block him! "

The scores of spectators lining the sides of the field were watching with keenest interest.

It was rumored that Dave and Dan had some new trick play hidden up their sleeves.

Yet, with two men squarely in the path of Darrin it seemed incredible that he could get by, for the Rustlers had bunched their interference skillfully at this point.

"Darry will have to stop! " yelled a score of voices at once, as Dave bounded at his waiting opponents.

"Yah, yah, yah! "

"Wow! "

"Whoop! "

The spectators had been treated to a sight that they never forgot.

Just as Dave reached those who blocked him he seemed to falter. It was Dan Dalzell who bumped in and received the opposition alone. Dan went down under it, all glory to him!

But Dave, in drawing back as he had done, had stepped aside like lightning, and now he had gone so far that he had no opposing end to dodge.

Instead, he darted straight ahead, leaving all of the forward line of the Rustlers behind.

But there was the back field to meet!

As Dave shot forward, Jetson, too, smashed over the line, blocking the halfback who got in his way.

Straight over the line charged Dave Darrin, and laid the ball down.

Now the athletic field resounded with excited yells. Annapolis had seen "a new one, " and it caught the popular fancy like lightning.

Back the pigskin was carried, and placed for the kick.

"You take it, Darry, " called Wolgast. "You've earned it! "

"Take it yourself, Wolly, " replied Dave Darrin. "This is your strong point. "

So Wolgast kicked and scored. The Rustlers at first looked dismayed over it all, but in another instant a cheer had broken loose from them.

It was the business of the Rustlers to harry the Navy team all they could—-to beat the Navy, if possible, for the Rustlers received their name from the fact that they were expected to make the team members rustle to keep their places.

Just the same the Rustlers were delighted to find themselves beaten by a trick so simple and splendid that it fairly took their breath away. For it was the Navy team, not the Rustlers, who met the enemy from the colleges and from West Point. Rustlers and team men alike prayed for the triumph of the Navy in every game that was fought out.

"You never told me that you had that trick, Darry, " muttered Wolgast, in the rest that followed this swift, brilliant play.

"I wanted to show it to you before telling you about it" laughed Dave.

"Why? "

"Because I didn't know whether it were any good. "

"Any good? Why, Darry, if you can get up one or two more like that you'll be the greatest gridiron tactician that the Navy has ever had! "

"I didn't get up that one, " Dave confessed modestly.

"You didn't, Mr. Darrin? " interposed Coach Parker. "Who did? "

"Mr. Jetson, sir. "

"I helped a bit, " admitted Jetson, turning red as he found himself the center of admiring gazes. "Dalzell and Darrin helped work it out, too. "

"Have you any more like that one, Mr. Darrin? " questioned Coach Parker.

"I think we have a few, sir, " Dave smiled steadily.

"Are you ready to exhibit them, Mr. Darrin? "

"We'll show 'em all, if you order it, sir, " Darrin answered respectfully. "But we'll undoubtedly spring two or three of 'em, anyway, in this afternoon's practice. "

"I'll be patient, then, " nodded coach. "But I want a brief talk with you after practice, Mr. Darrin. "

"Very good, sir. "

"I just want you to sketch out the new plays to me in private, that I may consider them, " explained the lieutenant-commander.

"Yes, sir. But I am not really the originator of any of the new plays. Mr. Dalzell and Mr. Jetson have had as much to do with all of the new ones as I have, sir. "

"And this is Darrin's last year! The Navy will never have his like again, " groaned one fourth classman to another.

"Ready to resume play! " called coach. "Navy to start the ball. "

The play was on again, in earnest, but this time it fell to the right flank of, the Navy team to stop the onward rush of the Rustlers as they charged down with the ball after the Navy's kick-off.

In fact, not during the team practice did Dave or Dan get a chance to show another of their new tricks.

"Just our luck! " grunted many of the spectators.

Meanwhile Dave, Dan and Jet got out of their togs, and through with their shower baths as quickly as they could, for Lieutenant-Commander Parker was on hand, awaiting them impatiently.

Until close to supper call did the coach hold converse with these three men of the Navy's left flank. Then the lieutenant-commander went to Midshipman Wolgast, who was waiting.

"Mr. Wolgast, I see the Army's banner trailed low in the dust this year, " laughed coach. "These young gentlemen have been explaining to me some new plays that will cause wailing and gnashing of teeth at West Point. "

"I'm afraid, sir, that you forget one thing, " smiled Darrin.

"What is that, sir? " demanded coach.

"Why, sir, the Army has Prescott and Holmes, beyond a doubt, for they played last year. "

"I saw Prescott and Holmes last year, " nodded Mr. Parker. "But they didn't have a thing to compare with what you've just been explaining to me. "

"May I remark, sir, that that was last year? " suggested Dave.

"Then you think that Prescott and Holmes may have developed some new plays. "

"I'd be amazed, sir, if they hadn't done so. And I've tried to have the Navy always bear in mind, sir, that Dalzell and myself learned everything we know of football under Dick Prescott, who, for his weight, I believe to be the best football player in the United States! "

"You're not going to get cold feet, are you, Mr. Darrin? " laughed Lieutenant-Commander Parker.

"No, sir; but, on the other hand, I don't want to underestimate the enemy. "

"You don't seem likely to commit that fault, Mr. Darrin. For my part, " went on coach, "I'm going to feel rather satisfied that Prescott and Holmes, of the Army, won't be able to get up anything that will equal or block the new plays you've been describing to me. "

Dave and Dan were more than usually excited as they lingered in their room, awaiting the call to supper formation. Farley and Page, all ready to respond to the call, were also in the room.

"I hope old Dick and Greg haven't got anything new that will stop us! " glowed Dan Dalzell.

"It's just barely possible, of course, " assented Darrin, "that they haven't. "

"If they haven't, " chuckled Farley gleefully, "then we scuttle the Army this year. "

"Wouldn't it be truly great, " laughed Page, "to see the great Prescott go down in the dust of defeat. Ha, ha! I can picture, right now, the look of amazement on his Army face! "

"We mustn't laugh too soon, " Dave warned his hearers.

"Don't you want to see the redoubtable Prescott shoved into the middle of next year? " challenged Midshipman Page.

"Oh, yes; of course. Yet that's not because he's Prescott, for good old Dick is one of the most precious friends I have in the world, " Dave answered earnestly. "I want to see Prescott beaten this year, and I want to have a hand in doing it--simply for the greater glory of the Navy! "

"Well, " grunted Page, "that's good enough for me. "

"We'll trail Soldier Prescott in the dust! " was a gleeful boast that circulated much through the Naval Academy during the few succeeding days.

Even Dave became infected with it, for he was a loyal Navy man to the very core. He began to think much of every trick of play that could possibly help to retire Dick Prescott to the background--all for the fame of the Navy and not for the hurt of his friend.

Dave even dreamed of it at night.

As for Dalzell, he caught the infection, proclaiming:

"We're out, this year, just to beat old Prescott and Holmes! "

Yet readers of the High School Boys' Series, who know the deep friendship that had existed, and always would, between Prescott and Holmes on the one side, and Darrin and Dalzell, on the other, do not need to be told that this frenzied feeling had in it nothing personal.

"If you two go on, " laughed Midshipman Farley, one evening after release, "you'll both end up with hating your old-time chums. "

"Don't you believe it! " retorted Dave Darrin almost sharply. "This is just a matter between the two service academies. What we want is to show the country that the Navy can put up an eleven that can walk all around the Army on Franklin Field. "

"A lot the country cares about what we do! " laughed Page.

"True, " admitted Dare. "A good many people do seem to forget that there are any such American institutions as the Military and the Naval Academies. Yet there are thousands of Americans who are patriotic enough to be keenly interested in all that we do. "

"This is going to be a bad year for Army friends, " chuckled Farley.

"And for the feelings of Cadets Prescott and Holmes, " added Page with a grimace.

As the practice went on the spirits of the Navy folks went up to fever heat. It was plain that, this year, the Navy eleven was to make history in the world of sports.

"Poor old Dick! " sighed Darrin one day, as the members of the squad were togging to go on to the field.

"Why? " Dan demanded.

"Because, in spite of myself, I find that I am making a personal matter of the whole business. Dan, I'm obliged to be candid with myself. It has come to the point that it is Prescott and Holmes that I want to beat! "

"Same case here, " Dan admitted readily. "They gave us a trouncing last year, and we're bound to pass it back to 'em. "

"I believe I'd really lose all interest in the game, if Dick and Greg didn't play on the Army this year. "

"I think I'd feel the same way about it, " agreed Dan. "But never fear—-they will play. "

Two days later Dan finished his bath and dressing, after football practice, to find that Dave had already left ahead of him. Dan followed to their quarters in Bancroft Hall, to find Dave pacing the floor, the picture of despair.

"Dan! " cried Darrin sharply. "This letter is from Dick. He doesn't play this year! "

"Don't tell me anything funny, like that, when I've got a cracked lip, " remonstrated Midshipman Dalzell.

"Dick doesn't play, I tell you—-which means that Greg won't, either. A lot of boobs at the Military Academy have sent Dick to Coventry for something that he didn't do. Dan, I don't care a hang about playing this year—-we can't beat Prescott and Holmes, for they won't be there! "

CHAPTER IV

DAVE'S WORK GOES STALE

"Aye, you're not—-not joking? " demanded Dan Dalzell half piteously.

"Do you see any signs of mirth in my face? " demanded Dave Darrin indignantly.

Rap-tap! Right after the summons Midshipman Farley and Page entered the room.

"Say, who's dead? " blurted out Farley, struck by the looks of consternation on the faces of their hosts.

"Tell him, Dave, " urged Dan.

"Prescott and Holmes won't play on this year's Army team, " stated Darrin.

"Whoop! " yelled Farley gleefully. "And that was what you're looking so mighty solemn about? Cheer up, boy! It's good news. "

"Great! " seconded Midshipman Page with enthusiasm.

"I tell you, fellows, " spoke Dave solemnly, "it takes all the joy out of the Army-Navy game. "

"Since when did winning kill joy? " demanded Farley aghast. "Why, with Prescott and Holmes out of it the Navy will get a fit of crowing that will last until after Christmas! "

"It makes the victory too cheap, " contended Darrin.

"A victory is a victory, " quoth Midshipman Page, "and the only fellow who can feel cheap about it is the fellow who doesn't win. Cheer up, Davy. It's all well enough to wallop a stray college, here and there, but the one victory that sinks in deep and does our hearts good is the one we carry away from the Army. Whoop! I could cry for joy. "

"But why won't Prescott and Holmes play this year? " asked Farley, his face radiant with the satisfaction that the news had given him.

"Because the corps has sent Prescott to Coventry for something that I'm certain the dear old fellow never did, " Darrin replied.

"Lucky accident! " muttered Farley.

"But the corps will repent, when they find their football hope gone, " predicted Page, his face losing much of its hitherto joyous expression.

"No! No such luck, " rejoined Midshipman Darrin. "If the brigade, here, sent a fellow to Coventry for what they considered cause, do you mean to tell me that they'd take the fellow out of Coventry just to get a good player on the eleven? "

"No, of course, not, " Page admitted.

"Then do you imagine that the West Point men are any more lax in their views of corps honor? " pressed Dave.

"To be sure they are not—-they can't be. "

"Then there's only a chance in a thousand that Dick Prescott will, by any lucky accident, be restored to favor in the corps—-at least, in time to play on this year's eleven. If he doesn't play, Holmes simply won't play. So that takes all the interest out of this year's Army-navy game. "

"Not if the Navy wins, " contended Midshipman Page.

"Bosh, there's neither profit nor honor in the Navy winning, unless it's against the best men that the Army can put forth, " retorted Dave Darrin stubbornly. "By the great Dewey, I'm afraid nine tenths of my enthusiasm for the game this year has been killed by the miserable news that has come in. "

Within less than five minutes after the midshipmen had seated themselves around the scores of tables in the mess hall, the news had flown around that Prescott and Holmes were to be counted as out of the Army eleven for this year.

Here and there suppressed cheers greeted the announcement The bulk of the midshipmen, however, were much of Dave Darrin's opinion that there was little glory in beating less than the best team that the Army could really put forth.

"Darry looks as though he had just got back from a funeral, " remarked one member of the third class to another youngster.

"I don't blame him, " replied the one so addressed.

"But he's all the more sure of winning over the Army this year. "

"I don't believe either of you youngsters know Darrin as well as I do, " broke in a second classman. "What I'm afraid of is, if Prescott and Holmes don't play with the soldiers, then Darry will lose interest in the game to such a degree that even Army dubs will be able to take his shoestrings away from him. Danny doesn't enjoy fighting fourth-raters. It's the big game that he enjoys going after. Why, I'm told that he had simply set his heart on pushing Prescott and Holmes all the way across Franklin Field this year. "

Readers who are anxious to know why Dick Prescott, one of the finest of American youths, had been sent to Coventry by his comrades at the United States Military Academy, will find it all set forth in the concluding volume of the West Point Series, entitled *"Dick Prescott's Fourth Year At West Point. "*

Strangely enough, the first effect of this news from West Point was to send the Navy eleven somewhat "to the bad. " That is to say, Dave Darrin, despite his best endeavors, seemed to go stale from the first hour when he knew that he was not to meet Dick Prescott on the gridiron.

"Mr. Darrin, what ails you? " demanded coach kindly, at the end of the second practice game after that.

"I don't know, sir. "

"You must brace up. "

"Yes, sir. "

"You seem to have lost all ambition. No; I won't just say that. But you appear, Mr. Darrin, either to have lost some of your snap or ambition, or else you have gone unaccountably stale. "

"I realize my defects, sir, and I am trying very, very hard to overcome them. "

"Are you ill at ease over any of your studies? " persisted coach.

"No, sir; it seems to me that the fourth year studies are the easiest in the whole course. "

"They are not, Mr. Darrin. But you have had the advantage of three hard years spent in learning how to study, and so your present course appears rather easy to you. Are you sleeping well? "

"Yes, sir. "

"Eating well? "

"Splendid appetite, sir. "

"Hm! I shall soon have a chance to satisfy myself on that point, Mr. Darrin. The day after to-morrow the team goes to training table. Have you any idea, Mr. Darrin, what is causing you to make a poorer showing? "

"I have had one very great disappointment, sir. But I'd hate to think that a thing like that could send me stale. "

"Oh, a disappointment? "

"Yes, sir, " Dave went on frankly. "You see, sir, I have been looking forward, most eagerly, to meeting Prescott and downing him with the tricks that Jetson, Dalzell and I have been getting up. "

"Oh! Prescott of the Army team? "

"Yes, sir. "

"I think I heard something about his having been sent to Coventry at the Military Academy. "

"But, Mr. Darrin, you are not going to fail us just because the Army loses a worthy player or two? " exclaimed Lieutenant-Commander Parker in astonishment.

"Probably that isn't what ails me, sir, " Dave answered flushing. "After all, sir, probably I'm just beginning to go stale. If I can't shake it off no doubt I had better be retired from the Navy eleven. "

"Don't you believe it! " almost shouted coach. "Mr. Darrin, you will simply have to brace! Give us all the best that's in you, and don't for one instant allow any personal disappointments to unfit you. You'll do that, won't you? "

"Yes, sir. "

Darrin certainly tried hard enough. Yet just as certainly the Navy's boosters shook their heads when they watched Darrin's work on the field.

"He has gone stale, " they said. "The very worst thing that could happen to the Navy this year! "

Then came the first game of the season—-with Lehigh. Darrin roused himself all he could, and his playing was very nearly up to what might have been expected of him—-though not quite.

The visitors got away with a score of eight to five against the Navy.

Next week the Lehighs went to West Point and suffered defeat at the hands of the Army.

The news sent gloom broadcast through the Naval Academy.

"We get beaten by one of the smaller colleges, that West Point can trim, " was the mournful comment.

It did, indeed, look bad for the Navy!

CHAPTER V

DAN HANDS HIMSELF BAD MONEY

As the season went on it was evident that Dave Darrin was slowly getting back to form.

Yet coach was not wholly satisfied, nor was anyone else who had the triumph of the Navy eleven at heart.

Three more games had been played, and two of them were won by the Navy. Next would come Stanford College, a hard lot to beat. The Navy tried to bolster up its own hopes; a loss to Stanford would mean the majority of games lost out of the first five.

True, the news from West Point was not wholly disconcerting to the Navy. The Army that year had some strong players, it was true; still, the loss of Prescott and Holmes was sorely felt. Word came, too, in indirect ways, that there was no likelihood whatever that the Coventry against Cadet Dick Prescott would be lifted. It was the evident purpose of the Corps of Cadets, for fancied wrongs, to ostracize Dick Prescott until he found himself forced to resign from the United States Military Academy.

November came in. Stanford came. Coach talked to Dave Darrin steadily for ten minutes before the Navy eleven trotted out on to the field. Stanford left Annapolis with small end of the score, in a six-to-two game, and the Navy was jubilant.

"Darrin has come back pretty close to his right form, " was the general comment.

For that Saturday evening Dan Dalzell, being now "on privilege" again, asked and received leave to visit in town—-this the more readily because his work on the team had prevented his going out of the Yard that afternoon.

Dave, too, requested and secured leave to go into town, though he stated frankly that he had no visit to make, and wanted only a stroll away from the Academy grounds.

Darrin went most of the way to the Prestons.

"Come right along through, and meet Miss Preston, " urged Dan.

"If you ask it as a favor I will, old chap, " Dave replied.

"No; I thought the favor would be to you. "

"So it would, ordinarily, " Darrin replied gallantly. "But to-night I just want to stroll by myself. "

"Ta-ta, then. " The grin on Dan Dalzell's face as he turned away from his chum was broader than usual. Dan was thinking that, this time, though his call must be a short one, he would be in no danger on his return. He could report unconcernedly just before taps.

"No doughface need apply to-night, " chuckled Dan. "But Davy was surely one awfully good fellow to get me through that other scrape as he did. "

All thought of football fled from Dan Dalzell's brain as he pulled the bellknob at the Preston house.

After all this was to be but the third meeting. Dan fancied, however, that absence had made his heart fonder. Since the night when he had Frenched it over the wall Dan had received two notes from Miss Preston, in answer to his own letters, but the last note was now ten days' old.

"May I see Mrs. Preston? " asked Dan, as a colored servant opened the door and admitted him.

This was Dan's correct idea of the way to call on a young woman to whom he was not engaged, but half hoped to be, some day.

The colored maid soon came back.

"Mrs. Preston is so very busy, sah, that she asks to be excused, sah, " reported the servant, coming into the parlor where Dan sat on the edge of a chair. "But Mistah Preston will be down right away, sah. "

A moment later a heavier step was heard on the stairway. Then May Preston's uncle came into the parlor.

"You will pardon Mrs. Preston not coming down stairs to-night, I know, Mr. Dalzell, " said the man of the house, as he and the midshipman shook hands. "The truth is, we are very much occupied to-night. "

"I had not dreamed of it, or I would not have called, " murmured Dan reddening. "I trust you will pardon me. "

"There is no need of pardon, for you have not offended, " smiled Mr. Preston. "I shall be very glad to spare you half an hour, if I can interest, you. "

"You are very kind, sir, " murmured Dan. "And Miss Preston— —"

"My niece? "

"Yes, sir. "

"It is mainly on my niece's account that we are so busy to-night, " smiled the host.

"She is not ill, sir? " asked Dan in alarm.

"Ill! Oh, dear me, no! "

Mr. Preston laughed most heartily.

"No; she is not in the least ill, Mr. Dalzell, though, on Monday, she may feel a bit nervous toward noon, "

"Nervous—-on Monday? " asked Dan vaguely. It seemed rank nonsense that her uncle should be able to predict her condition so definitely on another day.

"Why, yes; Monday is to be the great day, of course. "

"Great day, sir? And why 'of course'? " inquired Dan, now as much interested as he was mystified.

"Why, my niece is to be married Monday at high noon. "

"Married? " gasped Midshipman Dalzell, utterly astounded and discomfited by such unlooked-for news.

"Yes; didn't you know Miss Preston was engaged to be married? "

"I—-I certainly did not, " Dan stammered.

"Why, she spoke to you much of 'Oscar'———"

"Her brother? "

"No; the man who will be her husband on Monday, " went on Mr. Preston blandly. Being quite near-sighted the elder man had not discovered Dan's sudden emotion. "That is what occupies us to-night. We leave on the first car for Baltimore in the morning. Mrs. Preston is now engaged over our trunks. "

"I—-I am very certain, then, that I have come at an unseasonable time, " Dan answered hastily. "I did not know—-which fact, I trust, will constitute my best apology for having intruded at such a busy season, Mr. Preston. "

"There has been no intrusion, and therefore no apology is needed, sir, " replied Mr. Preston courteously.

Dan got out, somehow, without staggering, or without having his voice quiver.

Once in the street he started along blindly, his fists clenched.

"So that's the way she uses me, is it? " he demanded of himself savagely. "Plays with me, while all the time the day for her wedding draws near. She must be laughing heartily over—-my greenness! Oh, confound all girls, anyway! "

It was seldom that Midshipman Dalzell allowed himself to get in a temper. He had been through many a midshipman fight without having had his ugliness aroused. But just now Dan felt humiliated, sore in spirit and angry all over—-especially with all members of the gentler sex.

He even fancied that Mr. Preston was at that moment engaged in laughing over the verdant midshipman. As a matter of fact, Mr. Preston was doing nothing of the sort. Mr. Preston had not supposed that Dan's former call had been intended as anything more than a pleasant social diversion. The Prestons supposed that every one knew that their niece was betrothed to an excellent young fellow. So, at this particular moment, Mr. Preston was engaged in sitting on a trunk, while his wife tried to turn the key in the lock. Neither of them was favoring Midshipman Dalzell with as much as a thought.

"Why on earth is it that all girls are so tricky? " Dan asked himself savagely, taking it for granted that all girls are "tricky" where admirers are concerned.

"Oh, my, what a laugh Davy will have over me, when he hears! " was Dan's next bitter thought, as he strode along.

Having just wronged all girls in his own estimation of them, Dan was now proceeding to do his own closest chum an injustice. For Dave Darrin was too thorough a gentleman to laugh over any unfortunate's discomfiture.

"What a lucky escape I had from getting better acquainted with that girl! " was Dalzell's next thought. "Why, with one as wholly deceitful as she is there can be no telling where it would all have ended. She might have drawn me into troubles that would have resulted in my having to leave the service! "

Dan had not the least desire to do any one an injustice, but just now he was so astounded and indignant that his mind worked violently rather than keenly.

"Serves me right! " sputtered Dalzell, at last. "A man in the Navy has no business to think about the other sex. He should give his whole time and thought to his profession and his country. That's what I'll surely do after this. "

Having reached this conclusion, the midshipman should have been more at peace with himself, but he wasn't. He had been sorely, even if foolishly wounded in his own self esteem, and it was bound to hurt until the sensation wore off.

"You'll know more, one of these days, Danny boy, " was his next conclusion. "And what you know will do you a lot more good, too, if it doesn't include any knowledge whatever of girls—-except the disposition and the ability to keep away from 'em! I suppose there are a few who wouldn't fool a fellow in this shameless way but it will be a heap safer not to try to find any of the few! "

Dan's head was still down, and he was walking as blindly as ever, when he turned a corner and ran squarely into some one.

"Why don't you look out where you're going? " demanded that some one.

"Why don't you look out yourself? " snapped Midshipman Dalzell, and the next instant a heavy hand was laid upon him.

CHAPTER VI

THE "FORGOT" PATH TO TROUBLE

"Here, confound you! I'll teach you to— —-"

"Teach me how to walk the way you were going when I stopped you? " demanded the same voice, and a harder grip was taken on Dalzell's shoulder.

In his misery Dan was not at all averse to fighting, if a good excuse were offered. So his first move was not to look up, but to wrest him self out of that grip, haul away and put up his guard.

"Dave Darrin! " gasped Midshipman Dan, using his eyes at last.

Dave was laughing quietly.

"Danny boy, you shouldn't cruise without lights and a bow watch! " admonished Dave. "What sent your wits wool gathering? You look terribly upset over something. "

"Do I? " asked Dan, looking guilty.

"You certainly do. And see here, is this the way to the Preston house? "

"No; it's the way away from it. "

"But you had permission to visit at the Prestons. "

"That isn't any news to me, " grunted Dalzell.

"Then—-pardon me—-but why aren't you there? "

"Are you the officer of the day? " demanded Dan moodily.

"No; merely your best friend. "

"I beg your pardon, Dave. I am a grouch tonight. "

"Wasn't Miss Preston at home. "

"I—-I don't know. "

"Don't know? Haven't you been there? "

"Yes; but I didn't ask— —-"

As Dan hesitated Dave rested both hands on his chum's shoulders, looking sharply into that young man's eyes.

"Danny, you act as though you were *loco*. (crazy). What on earth is up? You went to call on Miss Preston. You reached the house, and evidently you left there again. But you don't know whether Miss Preston was in; you forgot to ask. Let me look in at the answer to the riddle. "

"Dave—-Miss Preston is going to be married! "

"Most girls are going to be, " Darrin replied quietly. "Do you mean that Miss Preston is going to marry some one else than yourself? "

"Yes. "

"Soon? "

"Monday noon. "

Dave Darrin whistled.

"So this is the meaning of your desperation? Danny boy, if you're stung, I'm sincerely sorry for you. "

"I don't quite know whether I want any sympathy, " Dan replied, though he spoke rather gloomily. "Perhaps I'm to be congratulated. "

He laughed mirthlessly, then continued:

"When a girl will treat a fellow like that, isn't it just as well to find out her disposition early? "

"Perhaps, " nodded Darrin. "But Danny, do you mean to say that you attempted to pay your call without an appointment? "

"What was the need of an appointment? " demanded Dan. "Miss Preston invited me to call at any time—-just drop in. Now, she must know that Saturday evening is a midshipman's only chance at this time of the year. "

"Nevertheless, you were wrong at that point, in the game, " Dave went on gravely. "Unless you're on the best of terms with a young lady, don't attempt to call on her without having learned that your purpose will be agreeable to her. And so Miss Preston, while receiving your calls, has been engaged to some one else? "

Dan nodded, adding, "She might have given me some hint, I should think. "

"I don't know about that, " Darrin answered thoughtfully. "Another good view of it would be that a young lady's private affairs are her own property. Didn't she ever mention the lucky fellow to you? "

"It seems that she did, " Dalzell assented. "But I thought, all the time, that she was talking about her brother. "

"Why should you especially think it was her brother whom she was mentioning? "

"Because she seemed so mighty fond of the fellow, " Dan grunted.

Dave choked a strong impulse to laugh.

"Danny boy, " he remarked, "girls, very often, are mighty fond, also, of the fellow to whom they're engaged. "

"Why did she let me call? " demanded Dan gloomily.

"How often have you called? " inquired Midshipman Darrin.

"Once, before to-night. "

"Only once? Then, see here, Danny! Don't be a chump. When you call on a girl once, and ask if you may call some other time, how on earth is she to guess that you're an intended rival of the man she has promised to marry? "

"But———" That was as far as Midshipman Dalzell got. He halted, wondering what he really could say next.

"Dan, I'm afraid you've got an awful lot to learn about girls, and also about the social proprieties to be observed in calling on them. As to Miss Preston receiving a call from you, and permitting you to call again, that was something that any engaged girl might do properly enough. Miss Preston came to Annapolis, possibly to learn something about midshipman life. She met you and allowed you to call. Very likely she permitted others to call. From what you've told me I can't see that she treated you unfairly in any way; I don't believe Miss Preston ever guessed that you had any other than the merest social reasons for calling. "

"And I'm not sure that I did have, " grunted Dalzell.

Dave shot another swift look into his chum's face before he said:

"Danny boy, your case is a light one. You'll recover speedily. Your vanity has been somewhat stung, but your heart won't have a scar in three days from now. "

"What makes you think you know so much about that? " insisted Dan, drawing himself up with a dignified air.

"It isn't hard to judge, when it's another fellow's case, " smiled Darrin. "I believe that, at this minute, I understand your feelings better than you do yourself. "

"I don't know about my feelings, " proclaimed Dan gloomily still, "but I do know something about my experience and conclusions. No more girls for me! "

"Good idea, Danny boy, " cried Darrin, slapping his friend on the back. "That's the best plan for you, too. "

"Why? "

"Because you haven't head enough to understand girls and their ways. "

"I don't want to. "

"Good! I hope you will keep in that frame of mind. And now, let's talk of something serious."

"Of what, then?" inquired Dalzell, as the two started to walk along together.

"Football."

"Is that more serious than girls?" demanded Dan Dalzell, suspicious that his friend was making fun of him.

"It's safer, at any rate, for you. Why, if a girl happens to say, 'Delighted to meet you, Mr. Dalzell,' you expect her to give up all other thoughts but you, and to be at home every Saturday evening. No, no, Danny. The company of the fair is not for you. Keep to things you understand better—-such as football."

Dan Dalzell's eyes shot fire. He was certain, now, that his chum was poking fun at him, and this, in his present temper, Dan could not quite endure.

"So, since we've dropped the subject of girls," Dave continued placidly, "what do you think are our real chances for the balance of this season?"

"They'd be a lot improved," grunted Dan, "if you'd get the grip on yourself that you had at the beginning of the season."

"I know I'm not playing in as good form as I had hoped to," Dave nodded. "The worst of it is, I can't find out the reason."

"A lot of the fellows think you've lost interest since you found that you won't have the great Prescott to play against in the Army-Navy game," Dan hinted.

"Yes; I know. I've heard that suspicion hinted at."

"Isn't it true?" challenged Dalzell.

"To the best of my knowledge and belief, it isn't. Why, Danny, it would be absurd to think that I couldn't play right now, just because Dick isn't to be against us on Franklin Field."

"I know it would sound absurd, " Dan replied. "But let us put it another way, Dave. All along you've been working yourself up into better form, because you knew that, otherwise, it was very doubtful whether the Navy could beat the Army on the gridiron. So you had worked yourself up to where you played a better game than ever Dick Prescott thought of doing. Then you hear that poor Dick is in Coventry, and therefore not on the team. You haven't got the great Army man to beat, and, just for that reason, you slack up on your efforts. "

"I am not slacking up, " retorted Dave with some spirit. "I am doing the best that is in me, though I admit I appear to have gone stale. "

"And so something will happen, " predicted Dan.

"What will that be? "

"Between now and the game with the Army, Prescott's comrades will find what boobs they've been, and they'll lift the Coventry. Prescott and Holmes will get into the Army team at the last moment, and the fellows from West Point will ride rough-shod over the Navy, just as they did last year. "

"Do you really think that will happen? " demanded Darrin eagerly. "Do you really believe that dear old Dick will get out of that Coventry and back on the Army eleven? "

"Well, " returned Midshipman Dalzell soberly, "I'll venture a prediction. If you don't get a brace on your playing soon, then it'll be regular Navy luck for Prescott to come to Philadelphia and put on his togs. Then the soldiers will drag us down the field to the tune of 46 to 2. "

"I'd sooner he killed on the field than see that happen! " cried Midshipman Dave, his eyes flashing.

"Then don't let it happen! You're the only star on our team, Dave, that isn't up to the mark. If we lose to the Army, this year, Prescott or no Prescott, it will be your fault, Dave Darrin. You're not one of our weak spots, really but you're not as strong as you ought to be and can be if you'll only brace. "

"Brace! " quivered Dave. "Won't I, though? "

"Good! Just stick to that."

"Dan!" Darrin halted his chum before a store where dry goods and notions were sold. "Let's go in here— —-"

"What, for?" Midshipman Dalzell asked in astonishment.

"I want to make a purchase," replied Dave soberly. "Danny boy, I'm going to buy you a hat pin—-one at least ten inches long. You're to slip it in, somewhere in your togs. When you catch me lagging—-practice or game—-just jab that hat pin into me as far as you can send it."

"Bosh!" retorted Dan impatiently. "Come along."

Dave submitted, in patient silence, to being led away from the store. For some moments the chums strolled along together in silence.

"Now, speaking of Miss Preston," began Dan, breaking the silence at last, "she— —-"

"Drop that! Get back to football, Danny—-it's safer," warned Dave Darrin.

"But— —-"

"Hold on, I tell you! You had almost recovered, Danny, in the short space of five minutes. Now, don't bring on a relapse by opening up the old sore. I shall soon begin to believe it was your heart that was involved, instead of your vanity."

"Oh, hang girls, then!" exploded Dan.

"Couldn't think of it," urged Dave gently. "That wouldn't be chivalrous, and even a midshipman is required to be a gentleman at all times. So— —-"

"Good evening, gentlemen," spoke a pleasant voice. The midshipmen glanced up, then promptly brought up their hands in salute to an officer whom they would otherwise have passed without seeing.

That officer was Lieutenant Adams, discipline officer.

"Are you enjoying your stroll, Mr. Darrin? " asked Mr. Adams.

"Very much, sir; thank you. "

"And you, Mr. Dalzell. But let me see—-wasn't your liberty for the purpose of paying a visit? "

"Yes, sir, " Dan answered, coloring.

"And you are strolling, instead? "

"Yes, sir; the person on whom I went to call was not there. "

"Then, Mr. Darrin, you should have returned to Bancroft Hall, and reported your return. "

"Yes, sir; I should have done that, " Dan confessed in confusion. "The truth is, sir, it hadn't occurred to me. "

"Return at once, Mr. Dalzell, and place yourself on report for strolling without permission. "

"Yes, sir. "

Both midshipmen saluted, then turned for the shortest cut to Maryland Avenue, and thence to the gate at the end of that thoroughfare.

"Ragged! " muttered Dan. "And without the slightest intention of doing anything improper. "

"It was improper, though, " Dave replied quickly, "and both you and I should have thought of it in time. "

"I really forgot. "

"Forgot to think, you mean, Dan, and that's no good excuse in bodies of men where discipline rules. Really, I should have gone on report, too. "

"But you had liberty to stroll in town. "

"Yes; but I'm guilty in not remembering to remind you of your plain duty. "

Lieutenant Adams had not in the least enjoyed ordering Dan to place himself on report. The officer had simply done his duty. To the average civilian it may seem that Dan Dalzell had done nothing very wrong in taking a walk when he found the purpose of his call frustrated; but discipline, when it imposes certain restrictions on a man, cannot allow the man himself to be the judge of whether he may break the restrictions. If the man himself is to be the judge then discipline ceases to exist.

"So I've got to stick myself on pap, and accept a liberal handful of demerits, all on account of a girl? " grumbled Dan, as the chums turned into the road leading to Bancroft Hall. "

"That is largely because you couldn't get the girl out of your head, " Dave rejoined. "Didn't I tell you, Danny, that you hadn't head enough to give any of your attention to the other sex? "

"It's tough to get those demerits, though, " contended Dan. "I imagine there'll be a large allowance of them, and in his fourth year a fellow can't receive many demerits without having to get out of the Academy. One or two more such scrapes, and I'll soon be a civilian, instead of an officer in the Navy! "

"See here, Dan; I'll offer an explanation that you can make truthfully. Just state, when you're called up, that you and I were absorbed talking football, and that you really forgot to turn in the right direction while your mind was so full of Navy football. That may help some. "

"Yes; it will—-not! "

Dan Dalzell passed into the outer room of the officer in charge, picked up a blank and filled it out with the report against himself.

Dave was waiting outside as Dan came out from the disagreeable duty of reporting himself.

"Hang the girls! " Dalzell muttered again disgustedly.

CHAPTER VII

DAN'S EYES JOLT HIS WITS

Dan Dalzell, on the point of stepping out of Bancroft Hall, wheeled like a flash, and bounded back against Farley, Jetson and Page.

"Don't look! " whispered Dan hoarsely. "Duck! "

"What on earth is the matter? " demanded Midshipman Darrin, eyeing his chum sharply.

"I—-I don't know what it is, " muttered Dan, after he had backed his friends some feet from the entrance.

"What does it look like? " asked Farley.

"Something like a messenger boy, " returned Dan.

"Surely, you're not afraid of a messenger boy with a telegram, " laughed Darrin. "Little chance that the message is for you, at any rate. "

"But—-it's got a Naval uniform on, I tell you, " warned Dan.

"No; you hadn't told us. What is it—-another midshipman? "

"Not by a jugful! " Dan sputtered. "It's wearing an officer's uniform. "

"Then undoubtedly you chanced to glance at an officer of the Navy, " Darrin replied, sarcastically soothing. "Brace up, Dan. "

"But he's only a kid! " remonstrated Dan. "And he wear a lieutenant's insignia! "

"Bosh! Some officers are quite boyish-looking, " remarked Farley. "Come on out, fellows; I haven't forgotten how to salute an officer when I see one. "

The others, except Dan, started briskly for the entrance. As for Dalzell, he brought up the rear, grumbling:

"All right; you fellows go on out and see whether you see him. If you don't, then I'm going to report myself at hospital without delay. Really, I can't swear that I saw—-it. "

But at that moment the object of Dan's alarm reached one of the doors of the entrance of Bancroft Hall and stepped briskly inside.

This new-comer's glance fell upon the knot of midshipmen, and he glanced at them inquiringly, as though to see whether these young men intended to salute him.

Surely enough, the newcomer was decidedly boyish-looking, yet he wore the fatigue uniform and insignia of a lieutenant of the United States Navy. If he were masquerading, here was a dangerous place into which to carry his antics.

The five midshipmen brought their right hands hesitatingly to the visors of their uniform caps. The very youthful lieutenant smartly returned their salutes, half smiled, then turned, in search of the officer in charge.

"Scoot! Skip! Let's escape! " whispered Dan hoarsely, and all five midshipmen were speedily out in the open.

"Now, did you fellows really see—-it—-or did I have a delusion that I saw you all salute when I did? "

"I saw it, " rejoined Farley, "and I claim it, if no one else wants it. "

"The service is going to the dogs, " growled Page, "when they give away a lieutenant's uniform with a pound of tea! "

"What ails you fellows? " rebuked Dave Darrin. "The man who passed us was a sure-enough lieutenant in the Navy. "

"Him? " demanded Midshipman Dalzell, startled out of his grip on English grammar. "A lieutenant? That—-that—-kid? "

"He's a lieutenant of the Navy, all right, " Dave insisted.

"You're wrong, " challenged Page. "Don't you know, Dave, that a man must be at least twenty-one years old in order to hold an officer's commission in the Navy? "

"That man who received our salutes is a Naval, officer, " Dave retorted. "I don't know anything about his age. "

"Why, that little boy can't be a day over seventeen, " gasped Dan Dalzell. "Anyway, fellows, I'm overjoyed that you all saw him! That takes a load off my mind as to my mental condition. "

"Whoever he is, he's a Navy officer, and he has trod the bridge in many a gale, " contended Dave. "Small and young as he looks, that man had otherwise every bit of the proper appearance of a Navy officer. "

"What a joke it will be on you, " grinned Page, "when you find the watchman dragging the little fellow away to turn over to the doctors from the asylum! "

The midshipmen were on their way to report for afternoon football work. As they had started a few minutes early, and had time to spare, they had now halted on the way, and were standing on the sidewalk in front of the big and handsome barracks building.

"Can you fellows still use your eyes? " Dave wanted to know. "If you can, look toward the steps of Bancroft. "

The officer in charge was coming out. At his side was the very youthful looking one in the lieutenant's uniform.

"The O. C. is decoying the stranger away to turn him over to the watchmen without violence, " guessed Midshipman Farley.

Three officers were approaching. These the five midshipmen turned and saluted. In another moment all of the five save Dave Darrin received a sharp jolt. For the O. C. had halted and was introducing the three Navy officers to the youthful one.

"This is Lieutenant Benson, the submarine expert of whom you have heard so much, " said the O. C., loudly enough for the amazed middies to hear.

"Sub—-sub——say, did you fellows hear that? " begged Dan hoarsely.

"Yes, " assented Dave calmly. "And say, you fellows are a fine lot to be serving here. You all remember Mr. Benson. He was here last year—-he and his two submarine friends. We didn't see them, because our class didn't go out on the Pollard submarine boat that was here last year. But you remember them, just the same. You remember, too, that Mr. Benson and his friends were hazed by some of the men in last year's youngster class. You heard about that? A lot of the fellows came near getting ragged, but Benson didn't take offense, and his quick wit pulled that lot of last year's youngsters out of a bad fix. "

"Then Benson and his mates are real people? " demanded Dan, still doubtful, if his voice were an indication.

"Yes; and Benson is a real submarine expert, too, even if he is a boy, " Dave went on.

"Then he is only a boy? "

"He's seventeen or eighteen. "

"Then how can he be a lieutenant? " demanded Dalzell, looking more bewildered.

"He isn't, " Dave answered simply.

"But the O. C. introduced him that way. "

"And quite properly, " answered Darrin, whereat his companions stared at him harder than ever.

"Let's walk along, " proposed Dave, "and I'll tell you the little that I know, or think I know, about the matter. Of course, you fellows all know about the Pollard submarine boats? The government owns a few of them now, and is going to buy a lot more of the Pollard craft. "

"But that kid officer? " insisted Dan.

"If you'll wait I'll come to that. Benson, his name is; Jack Benson he's commonly called. He and two boy friends got in on the ground floor at the Farnum shipyard. They were boys of considerable mechanical skill, and they found their forte in the handling of submarine boats.

They've done some clever, really wonderful feats with submarines. Farnum, the owner of the yard, trusted these boys, after a while, to show off the fine points of the craft to our Navy officers and others. "

"But what has that to do with giving Benson a commission in the Navy? " demanded Farley.

"I'm coming to that, " Dave replied. "As I've heard the yarn, Benson and his two boy friends attracted attention even from the European governments. The Germans and some other powers even made them good offers to desert this country and go abroad as submarine experts. Our Navy folks thought enough of Benson and his chums to want to save them for this country. So the Secretary of the Navy offered all three the rank and command of officers without the actual commissions. As soon as these young men, the Submarine Boys as they are called, are twenty-one, the Navy Department will bestir itself to give them actual commissions and make them real staff or line officers. "

"So that those kids will rank us in the service? " grumbled Dan.

"Well, up to date, " replied Dave quietly, "the Submarine Boys have done more for their country than we have. Of course, in the end, we may be admirals in the Navy, even before they're captains. Who can tell? "

"I wonder what Benson is doing here? " murmured Farley.

"Lieutenant Benson, " Dave corrected him, "is probably here on official business. If you want exact details, suppose we stop at the superintendent's house and ask him. "

"Quit your kidding, " grinned Farley.

"So I've got to say 'sir, ' if that boy speaks to me? " asked Dan.

"I think it would be better, " smiled Darrin, "if you're anxious to escape another handful of demerits. "

By the time that the football squad began to assemble on the football field, Dan and his friends found that some of the midshipmen were full of information about the famous Submarine Boys. Readers who may not be familiar with the careers of Lieutenant Jack Benson,

Ensign Hal Hastings, and Ensign Eph Somers are referred to the volumes of the *Submarine Boys' Series*. In *"The Submarine Boys and the Middies"* will be found the account of the hazing that Jack, Hal and Eph had received at the hands of midshipmen.

Benson and his two friends, with a crew of four men, were now at the Naval Academy, having arrived at two o'clock that afternoon, for the purpose of giving the first classmen instruction aboard the latest Pollard submarine, the "Dodger. "

But play was called, and that stopped, for the time being, all talk about the Submarine Boys.

CHAPTER VIII

THE PRIZE TRIP ON THE "DODGER"

The following afternoon, at the hour for instruction in the machine shops, the entire first class was marched down to the basin, where the "Dodger" lay. Squad by squad the midshipmen were taken on board the odd-looking little craft that was more at home beneath the waves than on them.

While the exact place and scale of importance of submarine war craft has not been determined as yet, boats of the Pollard type are certainly destined to play a tremendously important part in the Naval wars of the future. Hence all of the midshipmen were deeply interested in what they saw and were told.

Some of these first classmen were twenty-four years of age, others from twenty to twenty-two. Hence, with many of them, there was some slight undercurrent of feeling over the necessity for taking instruction from such very youthful instructors as Jack Benson, Hal Hastings and Eph Somers.

Had any of this latter trio been inclined to put on airs there might have been some disagreeable feeling engendered in the breasts of some of the middies. But Jack and his associates were wholly modest, pleasant and helpful.

Beginning on the following day, it was announced, the "Dodger" would take a squad of six midshipmen down Chesapeake Bay for practical instruction in submarine work, both above and below the surface of the water. This instruction would continue daily, with squads of six midshipmen on board, until all members of the first class had received thorough drilling.

"That's going to be a mighty pleasant change from the usual routine here, " whispered Farley in Dave's ear.

"It surely will, " Darrin nodded. "It will be even better fun than football. "

"With no chance for the Army to beat us out on this game, " Farley replied slyly.

At last it came the turn of Dave, Dan, Farley, Page, Jetson and Wolgast to go aboard the "Dodger. "

"Gentlemen, " announced Lieutenant Jack Benson, "Ensign Somers will show you all that is possible about the deck handling and the steering below the surface, and then Ensign Hastings will explain the mechanical points of this craft. When both are through, if you have any questions. I will endeavor to answer them. "

In a few minutes the "showing" had been accomplished.

"Any questions, gentlemen? " inquired Lieutenant Benson.

Dave was ready with three; Farley had four and Jetson two. Lieutenant Benson looked particularly pleased as he answered. Then, at last, he inquired:

"What's your name? "

"Darrin, sir, " Dave replied.

The other midshipmen present were asked their names, and gave them.

"Gentlemen, " continued youthful Lieutenant Benson, "this present squad impresses me as being more eager and interested in submarines than any of the squads that have come aboard. "

"Thank you, sir, " Dave replied for himself and the others.

"Are you really exceptionally interested? " inquired Benson.

"I think we are, sir, " Dave responded.

"On Saturday of each week, as long as the 'Dodger' is at Annapolis, " went on Benson, "we intend to take out one of the best squads. We shall drop down the Bay, not returning, probably before Sunday noon. Would you gentlemen like to be the first squad to go on the longer cruise—-next Saturday? "

The faces of all six midshipmen shone with delight for an instant, until Dave Darrin answered mournfully:

"It would give us great delight, sir, but for one thing. We play Creighton University next Saturday, and we are all members of the Navy team. "

"None of you look forward to having to go to hospital during the progress of the game, do you? " inquired Lieutenant Benson with a slight smile.

"Hardly, sir. "

"Then the 'Dodger' can sail an hour after the finish of the game, and perhaps stay out a little later on Sunday. Will that solve the problem? "

"Splendidly, sir! "

"Then I will use such persuasion as I can with the superintendent to have you six men detailed for the Saturday-Sunday detail this week, " promised Lieutenant Benson. "And now I will write your names down, in order that there may be no mistake about the squad that reports to me late next Saturday afternoon. Dismissed! "

As Dave and his friends stepped ashore even Dan Dalzell had a more gracious estimate of "that kid, Benson. "

That night, and for several nights afterwards, the "Dodger" and her officers furnished a fruitful theme for discussion among the midshipmen. As the "Dodger" was believed to be the very finest submarine craft anywhere among the navies of the world, the interest grew rather than waned.

Dave and Dan, as well as their four friends, began to look forward with interest to the coming cruise down the bay.

"Fellows, " warned Wolgast, "you'll have to look out not to get your heads so full of submarines that you lose to Creighton on Saturday. "

"On the contrary, " retorted Dave, "you can look for us to push Creighton all over the field. We'll do it just as a sheer vent to our new animal spirits. "

That was a decidedly boastful speech for Dave Darrin, yet on Saturday he made good, or helped tremendously, for Creighton retired from the field with the small end of an eight-to-two score.

"Now, hustle on the dressing, " roared Wolgast, as they started to un-tog and get under the showers, after the football victory.

"What's the need of rush? " demanded Peckham one of the subs.

"It doesn't apply to you, " Wolgast shot back over his shoulder, as he started on a run to the nearest shower. "I'm talking only to to-night's submarine squad. "

The six midshipmen found many an envious look shot in their direction.

"Those extremely youthful officers seem to have a bad case of spoons on you six, " remarked Peckham almost sourly.

"Show some nearly human intelligence, and maybe you'll get a chance at one of the Saturday cruises, Peckham, " called back Farley, as he began to towel down vigorously.

Dave and his friends were the first men of the team to be dressed and ready to leave.

"Give our best regards to Davy Jones! " shouted one of the football men.

"If you go down to the bottom of Chesapeake Bay, and can't get up again, don't do anything to spoil the fishing, " called another middy.

By this time Dave Darrin and his mates were outside and on their way to the basin.

Lieutenant Jack Benson was the only one of the "Dodger's" officers on view when the midshipmen arrived alongside. They passed aboard, saluting Benson, who returned their salutes without affectation.

"All here? " said Benson. "Mr. Somers, tumble the crew on deck! "

"Shall we go below, sir? " inquired Dave, again saluting.

"Not until so directed, " Benson replied. "I wish you to see every detail of the boat handling. "

At Lieutenant Jack's command the crew threw the hawsers aboard and soon had them out of the way.

Benson gave the starting signal to Eph Somers.

No sooner had the "Dodger's" hawsers been cast aboard than the submarine torpedo boat headed out. It was a get-away swift enough—-almost to take the breath of the midshipmen.

"You see, gentlemen, " Lieutenant Benson explained quietly, "we act on the theory that in submarine work every second has its value when in action. So we have paid a good deal of attention to the speedy start. Another thing that you will note is that, aboard so small a craft, it is important that, as far as is possible, the crew act without orders for each move. What do you note of the crew just now? "

"That they performed their work with lightning speed, sir, and that they have already gone below, without waiting for orders to that effect. "

"Right, " nodded Jack Benson. "Had the crew been needed on deck I would have ordered them to remain. As I did not so order they have gone below, where they are out of the way until wanted. A craft that fights always on the surface of the water should have some men of the crew always on deck. But here on a submarine the men would be in the way, and we want a clear range of view all over the deck, and seaward, in order that we may see everything that it is possible to see. Mr. Darrin, Mr. Dalzell and Mr. Farley will remain on deck with me. The other young gentlemen will go below to study the workings of the engines under Ensign Hastings. "

Though it was a true pleasure trip for all six of the midshipmen, it was one of hard, brisk instruction all the time.

"Here, you see, " explained Lieutenant Jack, leading his trio just forward of the conning tower, "we have a deck wheel for use when needed. Mr. Somers, give up the wheel. "

"Aye, aye, sir, " and Ensign Eph, who had been sitting at the tower wheel since the start, moved away and came on deck.

"Mr. Darrin, take the wheel, " directed Benson. "Are you familiar with the Bay? "

"Not sufficiently, sir, to be a pilot. "

"Then I will give you your directions from time to time. How does this craft mind her wheel? "

"With the lightest touch, sir, that I ever saw in a wheel. "

"The builders of the 'Dodger' have been working to make the action of the steering wheel progressively lighter with each boat that they have built. Men on a submarine craft must have the steadiest nerves at all times, and steady nerves do not go hand in hand with muscle fatigue. "

Lieutenant Jack walked to the entrance to the conning tower. "Mallock! " he called down to one of the crew.

"Aye, aye, sir. "

"My compliments to Mr. Hastings, and ask him to crowd the speed of the boat gradually. "

"Aye, aye, sir. "

The "Dodger" had been moving down the bay at a ten-knot pace. Suddenly she gave a jump that caused Midshipman Dave Darrin to wonder. Then the submarine settled down to a rushing sixteen-knot gait. "

"I didn't know, sir, " ventured Farley, "that submarines could go quite so fast. "

"The old types didn't, " Lieutenant Jack answered. "However, on the surface a capable submarine must be able to show a good deal of speed. "

"For getting away, sir? "

"Oh, no. Naturally, when a submarine is pursued she can drop under the surface and leave no trail. But suppose a single submarine to be guarding a harbor, unaided by other fighting craft. A twenty-or twenty-two knot battleship is discovered, trying to make the harbor. Even if the battleship steams away the submarine should be capable of following. The engines of the 'Dodger, ' in favorable weather, can drive her at twenty-six knots on the surface. "

"She's as fast as a torpedo-boat destroyer, then, sir, " hazarded Dan.

"Yes; and the submarine needs to be as fast. With the improvement of submarine boats the old style of torpedo boat will pass out altogether. Then, if the destroyer is retained the submarine must be capable of attacking the destroyer on equal terms. Undoubtedly, after a few years more the river gunboat and the submarine torpedo boat will be the only small fighting craft left in the navies of the leading powers of the world. "

Even while this brief conversation was going on the speed of the "Dodger" had begun to increase again. Ensign Hasting's head showed through the opening in the conning tower.

"We're going now at a twenty-knot clip, sir, " Hal reported. "Do you wish any more speed? "

"Not in Chesapeake Bay; navigating conditions are not favorable. "

"Very good, sir. " Hal vanished below. Never very talkative, Hal was content to stand by his engines in silence when there was no need of talking.

From time to time, as the craft sped on down the bay, Lieutenant Benson glanced at the chronometer beside the deck wheel.

"You don't have the ship's bell struck on this craft, sir? " inquired Midshipman Darrin.

"Only when at anchor or in dock, " replied Lieutenant Jack Benson. "A submarine's natural mission is one of stealth, and it wouldn't do to go about with a clanging of gongs. Now, let me have the wheel, Mr. Darrin. You gentlemen go to the conning tower and stand so that you can hear what goes on below. "

While the three midshipmen stood as directed the speed of the "Dodger" slackened.

Then, after a space of a full minute, the submarine returned to her former twenty-knot speed.

"Did you hear any clanging or jangling of a signal bell or gong when the speeds were changed? " questioned Lieutenant Benson.

"No, sir, " Darrin answered.

"That was because no bells were sounded, " explained Benson. "From deck or conning tower signals can be sent that make no noise. On a dark night, or in a fog, we could manoeuvre, perhaps, within a stone's throw of an enemy's battleship, and the only sound that might betray our presence would be our wash as we moved along. Take the wheel, Mr. Farley. "

Then, after giving Farley a few directions as to the course to follow, Lieutenant Benson added:

"Take command of the deck, Mr. Farley. "

"Humph! " muttered Dan. "The lieutenant doesn't seem to be afraid that we'll run his craft into any danger. "

"He knows as well as we do what would happen to me, if there were any disaster, and I had to explain it before a court of inquiry, " laughed Midshipman Farley. "Hello! Who slowed the boat down? "

Dan had done it, unobserved by his comrades, in an irrepressible spirit of mischief. He had reached over, touching the indicator, and thus directing the engine-room man to proceed at less speed. Dalzell, however, did not answer.

"I'd like to know if the speed were slackened intentionally, " fussed Farley. "Darry, do you mind going below and inquiring? "

"Not in the least, " smiled Dave, "but is it good Naval etiquette for one midshipman to use another midshipman as a messenger? "

"Oh, bother etiquette! " grunted Farley. "What would you really do if you were in command of the deck—-as I am—-and you wanted to ask a question, with the answer down below? "

"I'll go to the conning tower and summon a man on deck, if you wish, " Dave offered.

Farley nodded, so Dave stepped over to the conning tower, calling down:

"One man of the watch—-on deck! "

Seaman Mallock was on deck in a hurry, saluting Midshipman Farley.

"Mallock, report to Lieutenant Benson, or the next ranking officer who may be visible below. Report with my compliments that the speed of the craft has slackened, and inquire whether that was intentional. "

"Aye, aye, sir. "

Mallock was soon back, saluting.

"Engine tender reports, sir, that he slowed down the speed in obedience to the indicator. "

"But I—-—-" Farley began. Then he checked himself abruptly, noting out of the corner of his eye that Dan Dalzell had wandered over to the rail and stood looking off to seaward. If Dan were responsible for the slowing down of the speed, and admitted it under questioning, then Farley, under the regulations, would be obliged to report Dalzell, and that young man already had some demerits against his name.

"Oh, very good, then, Mallock, " was Midshipman Farley's rather quick reply. "Who is the ranking officer visible below at present? "

"Ensign Somers, sir. "

"Very good. My compliments to Mr. Somers, and ask at what speed he wishes to run. "

Seaman Mallock soon returned, saluting.

"Ensign Somers' compliments sir, and the ensign replies that Mr. Farley is in command of the deck. "

"Very good, then, " nodded Midshipman Farley, and set the indicator at the twenty mark.

Ten minutes later Lieutenant Benson reappeared on deck. First of all he noted the "Dodger's" position. Then, as Ensign Eph and Mallock appeared, Benson announced:

"Gentlemen, you will come down to Supper now. Mr. Somers, you will take command of the deck. "

"Very good, sir, " Eph responded. "Mallock, take the wheel. "

Lieutenant Benson seated himself at the head of the table, with Ensign Hastings on his right. The midshipmen filled the remaining seats.

"We're necessarily a little crowded on a craft of this size, " explained Benson. "Also the service is not what it would be on a battleship. We can carry but few men, so the cook must also act as waiter. "

At once a very good meal was set on the table, and all hands were busily eating when Eph Somers came down the stairs, saluted and reported:

"Sir, we are on the bottom of Chesapeake Bay, with our nose in the mud! "

CHAPTER IX

THE TREACHERY OF MORTON

To the midshipmen that was rather startling news to receive while in the act of enjoying a very excellent meal.

Lieutenant Jack Benson, however, appeared to take the news very coolly.

"May I ask, " he inquired, "whether any of you young gentlemen noticed anything unusual in our motion during the last two or three minutes? "

All six of the midshipmen glanced at him quickly, then at Darrin the other five looked, as though appointing him their spokesman.

"No, sir; we didn't note anything, " replied Dave. "We were too busy with our food and with listening to the talk. "

"But now you notice something? "

"Yes, sir. "

"What? "

"That the boat appears motionless, as though speed had been stopped. "

"And that is the case, " smiled Benson. "Mr. Somers, soon after the soup was placed on the table, came in from the deck with the one man of his watch, closed the tower and signaled for changing to the electric motors. Then he filled the forward tanks and those amidships, at last filling the tanks astern. We came below so gently that you very intent young men never noticed the change. We are now on the bottom--in about how many feet of water, Mr. Somers? "

"About forty, sir, " replied Eph.

The six midshipmen stared at one another, then felt a somewhat uncomfortable feeling creeping over them.

"Had it been daylight, " smiled Benson, "you would have been warned by the disappearance of natural light and the increased brilliancy of the electric light here below. However, your experience serves to show you how easily up-to-date submarines may be handled. "

"What do you think of the way the trick was done? " asked Hal Hastings, looking up with a quiet smile.

"It was marvelous, " replied Midshipman Farley promptly.

"I would like to ask a question, sir, if I may, " put in Midshipman Jetson.

"Go ahead, sir. "

"Were submarines ever handled anywhere near as neatly before you three gentlemen began your work with the Pollard Company? "

"We didn't handle them as easily, at all events, " replied Jack with a smile. "It has required a lot of work and practice, night and day. Steward, a plate for Mr. Somers. "

"This is the way we generally manage at meal times, " smiled Ensign Eph, as he took his place at table. "There's no use in keeping an officer and a man on deck, or a tender at the engines, unless we're going somewhere, in a hurry. So, in a case like this, where the deck officer wants his meal, we just sink into the mud and rest easy until the meal is over. "

"Are you giving instruction, or merely seeking to amuse your guests, Mr. Somers? " Lieutenant Jack Benson asked quietly.

"Oh, I forgot, " explained Eph, with another smile; "these young gentlemen are not yet acquainted with me. When they are they'll know that no one ever takes me too seriously. "

"A bad habit for a superior officer, isn't it? " inquired Benson, looking around at his student guests. "But Mr. Somers may be taken very seriously indeed—-when he's on duty. He is unreliable at table only. "

"Unreliable at table? " echoed Eph, helping himself to a slice of roast meat. "Why, it seems to me that this is the one place where I can be depended upon to do all that is expected of me. "

The others now sat back, out of courtesy, looking on and chatting while Ensign Eph Somers ate his meal. "There may be a few questions—-or many—-that you would like to ask, " suggested Lieutenant Jack Benson. "If so, gentlemen, go ahead with your questions. For that matter, during your stay aboard, ask all the questions you can think of. "

"Thank you, sir, " replied Midshipman Dave Darrin, with a slight bow. "I have been thinking of one point on which I would be glad of information. "

"And that is——-"

"The full complement of this craft appears to consist of three officers and four enlisted men—-that is, of course, outside of your combined cook and steward. "

"Yes, " nodded Benson.

"One of the officers is commanding officer; another is deck officer and the third engineer officer. "

"Yes. "

"Then, on a cruise, " pursued Dave, "how can you divide watches and thus keep going night and day? "

"Why, originally, " Jack replied, "we put on long cruises with only three aboard—-the three who are at present officers. With a boat like the 'Dodger, ' which carries so few men, the commanding officer cannot stand on his dignity and refuse to stand watch. I frequently take my trick at the wheel. That gives Mr. Somers his chance to go below and sleep. "

"Yet Mr. Hastings is your only engineer officer. "

"True, but two of our enlisted men are trained as engine-tenders. Our engines are rather simple, in the main, and an enlisted engine-tender can run our engine room for hours at a stretch under ordinary conditions. Of course, if anything out of the usual should happen while Mr. Hastings were taking his trick in his berth, he would have to be wakened. But we can often make as long a trip as from New York to Havana without needing to call Mr. Hastings once from his berth during his hours of rest. "

"Then you have two enlisted men aboard who thoroughly understand your engines? " pressed Dave Darrin.

"Ordinarily, " replied Hal Hastings, here breaking in. "But one of our engine-tenders reached the end of his enlisted period to-day, and, as he wouldn't re-enlist, we had to let him go. So the new enlisted man whom we took aboard is just starting in to learn his duties. "

"Small loss in Morton, " laughed Lieutenant Jack Benson. "He was enough of a natural genius around machinery, but he was a man of sulky and often violent temper. Really, I am glad that Morton took his discharge to-day. I never felt wholly safe while we had him aboard. "

"He was a bad one, " Ensign Hal Hastings nodded. "Morton might have done something to sink us, only that he couldn't do so without throwing away his own life. "

"I don't know, sir, what I'd do, if I were a commanding officer and found that I had such a man in the crew, " replied Midshipman Darrin.

"Why, in a man's first enlistment, " replied Lieutenant Jack, "the commanding officer is empowered to give him a summary dismissal from the service. Morton was in his second enlistment, or I surely would have dropped him ahead of his time. I'm glad he's gone. "

Ensign Eph had now finished his meal and was sitting back in his chair. Lieutenant Jack therefore gave the rising sign.

"I want to show the midshipmen everything possible on this trip, " said the very young commanding officer. "So we won't lie here in the mud any more. Mr. Somers, you will return to the tower steering wheel, and you, Mr. Hastings, will take direct charge of the engines. I will gather the midshipmen around me here in the cabin, and show the young gentlemen how easily we control the rising of a submarine from the bottom. "

Hal and Eph hurried to their stations. The midshipmen followed Jack Benson over to what looked very much like a switchboard. The young lieutenant held a wrench in his right hand.

"I will now turn on the compressed air device, " announced Lieutenant Jack. "First of all I will empty the bow chambers of water by means of the compressed air; then the middle chambers, and, lastly, the stern chambers. On a smaller craft than this we would operate directly with the wrench. On a boat of the 'Dodger's' type we must employ the wrench first, but the work must be backed up with the performance of a small electric motor. "

Captain Jack rapidly indicated the points at which the wrench was to be operated, adding:

"I want you to note these points as I explain them, for after I start with the wrench I shall have to work rapidly along from bow to stern tanks. Otherwise we would shoot up perpendicularly, instead of going up on a nearly even keel. Mr. Hastings, are you all ready at your post? "

"Aye, aye, sir, " came back the engineer officer's reply.

"On post, Mr. Somers? "

"Aye, aye, sir. "

Lieutenant Jack applied the wrench, calling snappily:

"Watch me. I've no time to explain anything now. "

With that he applied one of the wrenches and gave it a turn. Instantly one of the electric motors in the engine-room began to vibrate.

Almost imperceptibly the bow of the "Dodger" began to rise. Lieutenant Jack, intent on preserving an even keel as nearly as possible, passed on to the middle station with his wrench.

Just as he applied the tool the electric motor ceased running.

"What's the matter, Mr. Hastings? " Jack inquired quietly. "Something blow out of the motor? "

The submarine remained slightly tilted up at the bow.

"I don't know, sir, as yet, what has happened, " Hal Hastings answered back. "I'm going over the motor now. "

In a moment more he stepped into the cabin, a much more serious look than usual on his fine face.

"This, looks like the man Morton's work, " Hal announced holding a small piece of copper up before the eyes of the midshipmen. "Gentlemen, do you notice that the under side of this plate has been filed considerably? "

"Yes, sir, " nodded Dan Dalzell, a queer look crossing his face. "Won't the motor operate without that plate being sound? "

"It will not. "

The other midshipmen began to look and to feel strange.

"Then are we moored for good at the bottom of the bay? " asked Jetson.

"No; for we carry plenty of duplicate parts for this plate, " replied Ensign Hal. "Come into the engine room and I will show you how I fit the duplicate part on. "

Hal led the midshipmen, halting before a small work bench. He threw open a drawer under the bench.

"Every duplicate plate has been removed from this drawer, " announced Hastings quietly. "Then, indeed, we are stuck in the mud, with no chance of rising. Gentlemen, I trust that the Navy will send divers here to rescue us before our fresh air gives out! "

CHAPTER X

"WE BELONG TO THE NAVY, TOO! "

"You mean, sir, " asked Midshipman Jetson, his voice hoarse in spite of his efforts to remain calm, "that we are doomed to remain here at the bottom of the bay unless divers reach us in time? "

"Yes, " nodded Hal Hastings, his voice as quiet and even as ever. "Unless we can find a duplicate plate—-and that appears impossible—-the 'Dodger' is wholly unable to help herself. "

"If the outlook is as black as it appears, gentlemen, " spoke Jack Benson from behind their backs, "I'm extremely sorry that such a disaster should have happened when we had six such promising young Naval officers aboard. "

"Oh, hang us and our loss! " exploded Dave Darrin forgetting that he was addressing an officer. "I guess the country won't miss us so very much. But it surely will be a blow to the United States if the Navy's three best submarine experts have to be lost to the country to satisfy a discharged enlisted man's spite. "

Eph Somers had come down from the tower. He, too, looked extremely grave, though he showed no demoralizing signs of fear.

As for the six midshipmen, they were brave. Not a doubt but that every one of them showed all necessary grit in the face of this fearful disaster. Yet they could not conceal the pallor in their faces, nor could they hide the fact that their voices shook a little when they spoke.

"Make a thorough search, Mr. Hastings, " directed Lieutenant Jack Benson, in a tone as even as though he were discussing the weather. "It's barely possible that the duplicate plates have been only mislaid—-that they're in another drawer. "

Hal Hastings turned with one of his quiet smiles. He knew that the system in his beloved engine room was so exact that nothing there was ever misplaced.

"I'm looking, sir, " Hastings answered, as he opened other drawers in turn, and explored them. "But I'm not at all hopeful of finding the duplicate plates. This damaged one had been filed thinner, which shows that it was done by design. The man who would do that trick purposely wouldn't leave any duplicate plates behind. "

The four enlisted men and the cook had gathered behind their officers.

"Morton—-the hound! This is his trick! " growled Seaman Kellogg hoarsely. "Many a time I've heard him brag that he'd get even for the punishments that were put upon him. And now he has gone and done it—-the worse than cur! "

"No; there are no duplicate parts here, " announced Ensign Hastings at last.

"See if you can't fit on the old, worn one, " proposed Lieutenant Jack.

"No such luck! " murmured Hal Hastings. "Morton was too good a mechanic not to know bow to do his trick! He hasn't left us a single chance for our lives! "

None the less Hal patiently tried to fit the plate back and make the motor work, Lieutenant Jack, in the meantime, standing by the board with the wrench in hand. In the next ten minutes several efforts were made to start the motor, but all of them failed.

"And all for want of a bit of copper of a certain size, shape and thickness, " sighed Midshipman Dan Dalzell.

"It does seem silly, doesn't it, " replied Lieutenant Jack with a wan smile.

"At least, " murmured Midshipman Wolgast, "we shall have a chance to show that we know how to die like men of the Navy. "

"Never say die, " warned Ensign Eph Somers seriously, "until you know you're really dead! "

This caused a laugh, and it eased them all.

"Well, " muttered Jetson, "as I know that I can't be of any use here I'm going back into the cabin and sit down. I can at least keep quiet and make no fuss about it. "

One after another the other midshipmen silently followed Jetson's example. They sat three on either side of the cabin, once in a while looking silently into the face of the others.

Not until many minutes more had passed did the three officers of the "Dodger" cease their efforts to find a duplicate plate for the motor.

Kellogg and another of the seamen, though they met their chance of death with grit enough, broke loose into mutterings that must have made the ears of ex-seaman Morton burn, wherever that worthy was.

"I wish I had that scoundrel here, under my heel, " raged Seaman Kellogg.

"It will be wiser and braver, my man, " broke in Lieutenant Jack quietly, "not to waste any needless thought on matters of violence. It will be better for us all if every man here goes to his death quietly and with a heart and head free from malice. "

"You're right, sir, " admitted Kellogg. "And I wish to say, sir, that I never served under braver officers. "

"There won't be divers sent after us—-at least, within the time that we're going to be alive, " spoke Midshipman Farley soberly. "In the first place, Chesapeake Bay is a big place, and no Naval officer would know where to locate us. "

"Mr. Benson, " broke in Jetson suddenly, "I heard once that you submarine experts had invented a way of leaving a submarine boat by means of the torpedo tube. Why can't you do that now? "

"We could, " smiled Lieutenant Jack Benson, "if our compressed air apparatus were working. We can't do the trick without compressed air. If we had any of that which we could use, we wouldn't need to leave the boat and swim to the top. We could take the boat to the surface instead. "

"Then it's impossible, sir, to leave the boat? " questioned Jetson, his color again fading.

"Yes; if we opened the outer end of the torpedo tube, without being able to throw compressed air in there first, then the water would rush in and drown us. "

"I'm filled with wonder, " Dan Dalzell muttered to himself. "Staring certain death in the face, I can't understand how it happens that I'm not going around blubbering and making a frantic jackanapes of myself. There's not a chance of living more than an hour or two longer, and yet I'm calm. I wonder how it happens? It isn't because I don't know what is coming to me. I wonder if the other fellows feel just as I do? "

Dan glanced curiously around him at the other midshipmen faces.

"Do you know, " said Darrin quietly, "I've often wondered how other men have felt in just such a fix as we're in now. "

"Well, how do you feel, Darry? " Farley invited.

"I'm blessed if I really know. Probably in an instant when I fail briefly to realize all that this means my feeling is that I wouldn't have missed such an experience for anything. "

"You could have all my share of it, if I could make an effective transfer, " laughed Wolgast.

"If we ever do get out of this alive, " mused Page aloud, "I don't doubt we'll look back to this hour with a great throb of interest and feel glad that we've had one throb that most men don't get in a lifetime. "

"But we won't get out, " advanced Jetson. "We're up hard against it. It's all over but the slow strangling to death as the air becomes more rare. "

"I wonder if it will be a strangling and choking, " spoke Darrin again in a strange voice; "or whether it will be more like an asphyxiation? In the latter case we may drop over, one at a time, without pain, and all of us be finished within two or three minutes from the time the first one starts. "

"Pleasant! " uttered Wolgast grimly. "Let's start something—-a jolly song, for instance. "

"Want to die more quickly? " asked Dalzell. "Singing eats up the air faster. "

Lieutenant Jack Benson came out of the engine room for a moment. He took down the wrench and went back to the engine room. But first he paused, for a brief instant, shooting at the midshipmen a look that was full of pity for them. For himself, Jack Benson appeared to have no especial feeling. Then the young commanding officer went back into the engine room, closing the door after him.

"What did he shut the door for? " asked Jetson.

"Probably they're going to do something, in there, that will call for a good deal of physical exertion. "

"Well, what of that? " demanded Jetson, not seeing the point.

"Why, " Dave explained, "a man at laborious physical work uses up more air than a man who is keeping quiet. If the three officers are going to work hard in there then they've closed the door in order not to deprive us of air. "

"We called them kids, at first, " spoke Dan

Dalzell ruefully, "but they're a mighty fine lot of real men, those three acting Naval officers. "

Dave Darrin rose and walked over to the engine room, opening the door and looking in. Hal and Eph were hard at work over the motor, while Lieutenant Jack Benson, with his hand in his pockets, stood watching their efforts.

"I beg your pardon, sir, " said Darrin, saluting, "but did you close this door in order to leave more air to us? "

"Yes, " answered Jack Benson. "Go back and sit down. "

"I hope you won't think us mutinous, sir, " Darrin returned steadily, "but we don't want any more than our share of whatever air is left on board this craft. We belong to the Navy, too. "

From the after end of the cabin came an approving grunt. It was here that the cook and the four seamen had gathered.

With the door open the midshipmen could see what was going on forward, and they watched with intense fascination.

Eph Somers had taken 'the too-thin copper' plate to the work-bench, and had worked hard over it, trying to devise some way of making it fit so that it would perform its function in the motor. Now, he and Hal Hastings struggled and contrived with it. Every time that the pair of submarine boys thought they had the motor possibly ready to run Hal tried to start the motor. Yet he just as often failed to get a single movement from the mechanism.

"I reckon you might about as well give it up, " remarked Lieutenant Jack Benson coolly.

"What's the use of giving up, " Eph demanded, "as long as there's any life left in us? "

"I mean, " the young lieutenant explained, "that you'd better give up this particular attempt and make a try at something else. "

"All right, if you see anything else that we can do, " proposed Eph dryly. "Say, here's a quarter to pay for your idea. "

Seemingly as full of mischief as ever, Eph Somers pressed a silver coin into Jack Benson's hand.

But Jack, plainly impatient with such trifling, frowned slightly as he turned and pitched the quarter forward.

"This isn't a twenty-five-cent proposition, " Benson remarked. "In fact, all the money on earth won't save us this time! "

CHAPTER XI

A QUARTER'S WORTH OF HOPE

"Until some one can think of something else, I'm going to keep on trying the hopeless thing and endeavoring to make this old, thin plate work, " declared Hal Hastings, who was still bent over the motor, studying it intently.

Benson had turned back to examine the work, after tossing the coin away, but just as suddenly he glanced forward again.

At the extreme forward end of the engine room of the "Dodger" was another bench. Here were a vise and other heavier tools. On the floor under this bench were stowed many mechanical odds and ends-- pieces of wood, coils of rope, even a bundle of tent-pegs, though nothing was visible of a metallic nature.

"You fellows keep at work, " Jack Benson shot back suddenly over his shoulder.

"Where you going? " demanded Eph.

"Forward. "

That much was evident, but Jack was now down on hands and knees carefully yet feverishly moving the wooden articles, cordage and such things from under the forward bench.

"What are you doing? " called Eph. "Go ahead with your work-- there's no time to be lost, " replied Lieutenant Jack.

"Hold this a moment, Eph, " Hal Hastings requested, and Somers's attention was forced back to the motor.

Sc-cratch! Flare! Jack Benson was using matches under that work bench, now that be had made some clear space there.

"I wonder if Jack has gone clean daffy? " half chuckled Somers under his breath.

"What are you talking about? " Hastings demanded.

"Jack's lighting matches up forward, under the other bench. "

"What if he is? "

"Maybe he thinks he can explode some gasoline and blow us to the surface. "

"Quit your nonsense, " returned Hal almost angrily, "and help me with this job. "

"I'm waiting to see if Jack is going to let out a maniac yell, " grimaced Eph Somers.

"Quit your— —-"

"Wow! Whoop! " uttered young Benson excitedly. "Never tell me again that it's unlucky to throw money away! Whoop! "

"What did I tell you? " demanded Eph. "If Jack's making a noise like that, " retorted Hastings, as be straightened up and wheeled about, "he's got a mighty good reason for it. "

"Of course. Every lunatic has loads of good reasons for anything he does, " muttered Eph.

"Look here, fellows! " ordered Jack Benson, almost staggering as he approached them.

"Great Dewey! Am I going crazy, too? " muttered Eph, staring hard. "What I think I see in Jack's hands are some of the missing copper plates. "

"It's exactly what you do see, " announced Jack Benson, his face beaming.

"But how—-"

"How they came to be there I don't know, " Benson replied. "But when I threw away your quarter, Eph, it rolled under the bench. There wasn't supposed to be anything metallic under the bench, but I felt almost, sure that I had heard the silver strike against something metallic. Even then it seemed like a crazy notion to me. I didn't really expect to find anything, but some uncontrollable impulse urged me to go hustling under the bench. And so I found these duplicate plates, wedged in behind a lot of junk and right up against the partition. "

Hal Hastings, in the meantime, had taken one of the plates from Lieutenant Jack's hand, and was now quietly fitting it where it belonged on the motor.

The six midshipmen, as soon as they realized what had happened, had sprung eagerly to the door of the engine room and stood peering in. Behind them were the cook and crew of the "Dodger. "

Presently Hal straightened up.

"Sir, " he said gravely, "I have hopes that if you test the compressed air apparatus you will find that this motor will do its share. "

Midshipmen and crew drew back as Jack and Eph came out of the engine room. Lieutenant Jack had his wrench in hand, and went back to his former post.

"Young gentlemen, " the commanding officer announced coolly, "we will take up, at the point where we were interrupted, the work of expelling the water from the compartments Are you ready, Mr. Hastings? "

"Right by my post, sir, " came from Hal.

The six midshipmen gathered about Benson with a stronger sense of fascination than ever. Eph stepped past them to the stairs leading-- to the little conning tower.

With steady hand Jack Benson turned the wrench. The motor began to "mote" and there was a sense of being lifted.

"Going up! " sang Ensign Eph, with a grin.

Nor could Dan Dalzell help imitating the grin and calling out jovially:

"Let me out at the top floor, please! "

Having set the compressed air at work on the forward tanks, Jack Benson quickly shifted the wrench, and without a word, getting at work on the midship's compartments. Then the stern tanks were emptied.

"May I come up, sir? " called Dan, his voice trembling with joy, at the foot of the stairs.

"Very good, " Eph sang back. "Room for only one, though, "

So Dan Dalzell hastily mounted the iron stairs until he found himself side by side with Eph Somers.

For a few seconds all was inky darkness on the other side of the thick plate glass of the conning tower. Then, all in a flash, Dalzell caught sight of the twinkling stars as the dripping conning tower rose above the top of the water.

"I have the honor to report that all's well again, and that we're on earth once more, " Dan announced, as he came down the steps into the little cabin.

"Attention, gentlemen, " called Lieutenant Jack Benson, as soon as the "Dodger" was once more under way, her sea-going gasoline engines now performing the work lately entrusted to the electric motors.

At the word "attention" the six midshipmen became rigidly erect, their hands dropping at their sides.

"Gentlemen, " continued Benson, "I realize that the late strain has been a severe one on us all. We of the 'Dodger' have been through the same sort of thing before. You midshipmen have not. If you feel, therefore, that you would prefer to have me head about and return to the Naval Academy I give you my word that I shall not think you weak-kneed for making the request. "

"Thank you, sir, " replied Dave Darrin, "but we belong to the United States Navy and we have no business to suffer with nerves. If our wish alone is to be consulted, we prefer to finish the cruise as we would any other tour of duty. "

Dave's five comrades in the Brigade of Midshipmen loved him for that answer!

CHAPTER XII

READY TO TRIM WEST POINT

"Have had an experience, sir, that we shall never forget, and one that we wouldn't have missed! "

Thus spoke Dave Darrin the, following afternoon, as he saluted the young officers of the "Dodger" before going over the side as the boat lay alongside the wall of the basin.

To which the other midshipmen agreed.

"We have enjoyed having you aboard, " replied Lieutenant Jack Benson. "None of us will ever forget this cruise. "

Then the six midshipmen strode briskly along the walks until they reached Bancroft Hall.

It wasn't long ere news of the adventure of the night before got whispered along the decks. Then Dave and Dan, Farley and Page, Jetson and Wolgast all had so much midshipman company that it was a relief when the evening study hours came around.

All six of the midshipmen had to tell the story of their submarine experience until all of them fairly hated to talk about the matter. Seaman Morton was never heard from again, and so did not come in for his share of the excitement. However, it was not destined to last long, for the football season was at its height and every blue-clad middy thought, talked and dreamed about the Navy team.

A good team it was, too, and a good year for the Navy. The young men of the Naval Academy played one of their most brilliant seasons of football.

Dave, by a bigger effort than any one understood, forced back his interest in the gridiron until he played a brilliant game.

The Navy won more victories than it had done before in any one of fifteen seasons of football.

Yet report said that the Army, too, was playing a superb game, considering that it had been deprived of its two best players, Prescott and Holmes.

Up to the last Dave continued to hope that Cadet Dick Prescott might be restored to the Army eleven. Dick's letters from West Point, however, appeared to indicate clearly that he was not to play. Therefore Greg Holmes wouldn't play.

At last came the fateful day, the Saturday after Thanksgiving. Early the Brigade of Midshipmen was marched over to the trolley line, where a long string of cars waited to receive them.

"We want an extra car to-night, " one first classman called jovially to the car inspector who was in charge of the transportation. "We want that extra car to bring back the Army scalp in. "

All the way to Baltimore and thence to Philadelphia, Dave Darrin was unusually quiet. Dalzell, on the other hand, made noise enough for both of them.

"Darry hasn't the sulks over anything, has be? " Wolgast anxiously asked Dalzell.

"Don't you believe it, " Dan retorted.

"But he's so abominably quiet. "

"Saving all his breath to use on the field. "

"Are you sure Darry is in form? " persisted Wolgast.

"Yes. Wait and see. "

"I'll have to, " sighed Wolgast, with another sidelong glance at Darrin's emotionless face.

The Navy team and subs. arrived at dressing quarters nearly an hour before it would be necessary to tog.

As the West Point men were on hand, also, Dave stepped outside. Almost the first man he met was a tall, slim, soldierly looking fellow in the cadet gray.

"Aren't you Fields? " asked Dave, holding out his hand.

"Yes, " replied the cadet, giving his own hand.

"And you're Darrin—-one of the few men we're afraid of. "

"Does Prescott play to-day? " Dave asked eagerly.

The West Pointer's brow clouded.

"No, " he replied. "Mr. Prescott isn't a subject for conversation at the Military Academy. Mr. Prescott is in Coventry. "

"Sad mistake, " muttered Darrin.

"Eh? "

"A sad mistake. You men have made a bad bungle; I know it. "

"It is a matter of internal discipline in the corps, " replied the West Point cadet, speaking much more coldly.

"Yes, I know it, " Dave replied quickly, "and I beg your pardon for having seemed to criticise the action of the Corps of Cadets. However, anything that unpleasantly affects Dick Prescott is a sore subject with me. Prescott is one of the best friends I have in the world. "

"Why, I've heard something about that, " replied Fields in a less constrained tone. "You and Mr. Prescott are old school cronies. "

"Of the closest kind, " Dave nodded. "That's why I feel certain that Dick Prescott never did, and never could do, anything dishonorable. You'll surely find it out before long, and then the Corps will make full amends. "

"I fear not, " replied Cadet Fields. "Mr. Prescott had every opportunity given him to clear himself, and failed to do so to the satisfaction of the Corps. Therefore he'll never graduate from the Military Academy. It wouldn't do him any good to try. He'd only be ostracized in the Army if he had the cheek to stay in the Corps. "

"Let's not talk about that part of it any more, " begged Dave. "But you'll miss Prescott from your fighting line to-day. "

"That's very likely, " assented the West Point man. "I'm glad we haven't Mr. Prescott here, but we'd be heartily glad if we had some one else as good on the football field. "

"And you haven't Holmes, either? " sighed Dave.

"That isn't any one's fault but Holmesy's, " frowned Cadet Fields. "We wanted Holmesy to play, and we gave him every chance, but—-"

"But he wouldn't, " finished Dave. "No more would I play on the Navy team if the fellows had done anything unjust to Dalzell. "

"Do you feel that you're going to have an easy walk-over with us to-day? " demanded Cadet Fields cheerily.

"No; but we're prepared to fight. We'll get the game if it's in any way possible, " Darrin assured his questioner.

"Are the bonfires back in Annapolis all ready to be lighted to-night? " inquired Fields smilingly.

"They must be. "

"What a lot of unnecessary labor, " laughed the West Point man.

"Why? " challenged Dave.

"Because the Army is going to win again. " That "again" caused Dave Darrin to wince. "We win almost every time, you know, " Fields explained.

"Almost every time? " challenged Dan Dalzell, joining the pair. "Are you sure of your statistics? "

"Oh, I have the statistics, of course, " Fields answered. "That's why I speak so confidently. "

At this point three more West Point men approached.

"Hey, fellows, " called Fields good-humoredly. "Do you know of an impression that I find to prevail among the middies to-day? "

"What is that? " inquired one of the gray-clad cadets, as the newcomers joined the group.

"Why, the middies seem to think that they're going to take the Army's scalp to-day. "

"Is that really your idea of the matter? " asked one of the gray-clad cadets.

"So Mr. Fields has said, " Dave answered.

"But what do you say? "

"About the most that I feel like saying, " Darrin answered as quietly as ever, "is that the Navy prefers to do its bragging afterwards. "

"An excellent practice, " nodded one of the cadets. "You've acquired the habit through experience, I presume. It has saved your having to swallow a lot of your words on many occasions. "

All laughed good-naturedly. Though there was the most intense rivalry between the two government military schools, yet all were gentlemen, and the fun-making could not be permitted to go beyond the limits of ordinary teasing.

"What's your line-up? " broke in Dan Dalzell.

"Haven't you fellows gotten hold of the cards yet? " asked one of the West Point men. "Then take a look over mine. "

Standing together Dave and Dan eagerly glanced down the printed line-up of the Military Academy.

"I know a few of these names, " ventured Darrin, "and they're the names of good men. Several of the other names I don't know at all. And you've left out the names of the two Army men that we're most afraid of in a game of football. "

"It seems queer to think of an Army line-up without Prescott and Holmes, " Dan declared musingly.

Over the faces of the cadets there crept a queer look, but none of them spoke.

"So you've boycotted Prescott and Holmes? " pursued Dalzell.

"Yes, " replied one of the cadets. "Or, rather, Prescott is in Coventry, and Holmes prefers to stand by his friend in everything. Holmes, being Prescott's roommate, doesn't have to keep away from Mr. Prescott. "

"Humph! " laughed Dan. "I think I can see Greg Holmes turning his back upon Dick Prescott. Why, Greg wouldn't do that even if he had to get out of the Army in consequence. "

"We did the only thing we could with the Prescott fellow, " spoke up another cadet.

Dave Darrin's dark eyes flashed somewhat.

"Gentlemen, " he begged quietly, "will you do me the very great favor not to refer to Prescott slightingly as a 'fellow. ' He's one of the noblest youngsters I've ever known, and I'm his friend through thick and thin. Of course, I don't expect you to know it yet, but I feel positive that you've made a tremendous mistake in sending to Coventry one of nature's noblemen. "

"Hm! " muttered some of the cadets, and slight frowns were visible.

"And when you lose the game to-day, " continued Dan Dalzell, "it may be a comfort to you to know that you might possibly have won it if you had had Prescott and Holmes in your battle front. "

"Prescott isn't the only football player in the Army, " returned Cadet Fields. "Nor are he and Holmes the only pair of 'em. "

"You'll lose without that pair, though, " ventured Dave. "And it must shake the confidence of your men, too, for you've come here without your two best men. "

"Of course, we have to manage our own affairs, " interposed one of the cadets.

"Gentlemen, " spoke up Dave quickly, "of course, you have to manage your own problems, and no one else is fitted to do so. If I've gone too far in what might have seemed like criticism, then I beg you to forget it. I don't want to be suspected of any disagreeable intent. If I spoke almost bitterly it was because Prescott is my very dear friend. I have another, and a real grievance—-I wanted to test myself out today against Dick Prescott, as any two friends may contest to vanquish one another on the field of sports. "

"No one had any thought, I am sure, Mr. Darrin, of accusing you of wishing to be disagreeable, " spoke up Cadet Fields. "We believe you to be a prince of good and true fellows; in fact, we accept you at the full estimate of the Brigade of Midshipmen. Wade in and beat us to-day, if you can—-but you can't Prescott or no Prescott. "

"Better run inside and tog! " called Wolgast from a distance.

"You'll excuse us now, won't you? " asked Dave. "Come along, Danny boy. "

As the two midshipmen lifted their caps and hastened away, Fields gazed after them speculatively:

"There goes the Navy's strength in to-day's game, " he announced.

"I wonder if we have done Prescott any wrong? " said another cadet slowly.

"That question has been settled by formal class action, " replied another. "It's a closed matter. "

Then these West Point men strolled over to quarters to get into togs. As they were to play subs. they did not need to be as early at togging as the members of the team.

Out on Franklin Field thousands and thousands of Americans, from the President of the United States down, waited impatiently for the excitement of the day to begin.

On either side of the field some hundreds of seats were still left vacant. The music of a band now floated out, proclaiming that one set of seats was soon to be filled. Then in, through a gate, marched the Military Academy band at the head of the Corps of Cadets.

Frantic cheers broke loose on the air, and there was a great fluttering of the black and gray banners carried by the Army's boosters in the audience. Gray and steel-like the superb corps marched in across the field, and over to the seats assigned to them.

Barely had the Army band ceased playing when another struck up in the distance. It was now the turn of the fine Naval Academy band to play the Brigade of Midshipmen on to the field. Again the air vibrated with the intensity of the loyal cheers that greeted the middies.

Over in quarters, after the middies of the team had togged, a few anxious minutes of waiting followed. What was to be the fate of the day?

"Darry, " spoke Wolgast in a voice full of feeling, "you're not woozy to-day, are you? "

"I don't believe I am, " smiled Dave.

"Well, you know, old chap, you've been unaccountably stale—-or something—-at times this season. You haven't been the real Darry—-always. You're feeling in really bully form today? "

"I'm pretty sure that I'm in good winning form, " Dave replied. "Will that be enough? "

Wolgast looked him over, then rejoined:

"Somehow, I think you're in pretty good form. I'll feel better, very likely, after we've played for ten minutes. Darry, old fellow, just don't forget how much the Navy depends upon you. "

"Are you all right, Davy? " Dan Dalzell demanded in a more than anxious undertone.

"I certainly am, Danny boy. "

"But, you know——-"

"Yes; I know that, for a while, I showed signs of going fuzzy. But I'm over that. "

"Good! " chuckled Dan, as he caught the resolute flash in Darrin's eyes. "I was fearfully afraid that you'd go bad simply because you didn't have Prescott to go up against. For a good many days that very fact seemed to prey upon your mind and make you indifferent. "

"Danny boy, I am going to play my mightiest, just because Prescott isn't with the Army! "

"What do you mean by that? "

"I mean that I'm going to make the West Point fellows most abominably sorry that they didn't have Dick Prescott on their eleven. And you want to stand with me in that, Danny boy. Keep hammering the Army to-day, and with every blow just think it's another blow struck for Dick Prescott and Greg Holmes. Oh, we'll trim West Point in their joint name! "

CHAPTER XIII

WHEN "BRACE UP, ARMY! " WAS THE WORD

"All out for practice! " called Wolgast.

Team men and subs. bunched, the Navy players trotted on to the field, amid a tempest of wild cheering.

No sooner had Dave Darrin halted for an instant, when he broke into a whirlwind of sprinting speed. Dan Dalzell tried to keep up with him, but found it impossible.

"Good old Darry! " yelled a hoarse voice from one of the grandstands. "That's the way you'll go around the end to-day! "

Some of the other Navy players were kicking a ball back and forth. The Army team was not yet on the field, but it came, a few moments later, and received a tremendous ovation from its own solid ranks of rooters.

This time Darrin barely glanced at any of the Army players. He knew that Prescott and Holmes were not there. Whoever else might be, he was not interested.

Only a very few minutes were allowed for practice. During this exercise the Army and Navy bands played alternately.

Then the referee signaled the bands to stop.

Tril-l-l-l! sounded the whistle, and Army and Navy captains trotted to the center of the field to watch the toss of the coin. Wolgast won, and awarded the kick-off to the Army.

Then the teams jogged quickly to places, and in an instant all was in readiness.

Over the spectators' seats a hush had fallen. Even the Army and Navy cheer leaders looked nearly as solemn as owls. The musicians of the two bands lounged in their seats and instruments had been laid aside. There would be no more noise until one team or the other had started to do real things.

Quick and sharp came the signal. West Point kicked and the ball was in play.

Navy's quarterback, after a short run, placed himself to seize the arching pigskin out of the air. Then he ran forward, protected by the Navy interference.

By a quick pass the ball came into Dave Darrin's hands. Dalzell braced himself as he hit the strong Army line.

It was like butting a stone wall, but Darrin got through, with the aid of effective interference.

Army men bunched and tackled, but Dave struggled on. He did not seem to be exerting much strength, but his elusiveness was wonderful,

Then, after a few yards had been gained, Dave was borne to the earth, the bottom of a struggling mass until, the referee's whistle ended the scrimmage.

Annapolis players could not help shooting keen glances of satisfaction at each other. The test had been a brief one, but now they saw that Darrin was in form, and that he could be depended upon to-day, unless severe accident came to cripple him.

Again the ball was put in play, this time going over to Farley and Page on the right end.

Only a yard did Farley succeed in advancing the ball, but that was at least a gain.

Then again came the pigskin to the left flank, and Dave fought it through the enemy's battle line for a distance of eight feet ere he was forced to earth with it.

By this time the West Point captain was beginning to wonder what ailed his men. The cadet players themselves were worried. If the Navy could play like this through the game, it looked as though Annapolis might wipe out, in one grand and big-scored victory, the memory of many past defeats.

"Brace up, Army! " was the word passed through West Point's eleven.

"Good old Darry! " chuckled Wolgast, and, though he did not like to work Darrin too hard at the outset, yet it was also worth while to shake the Army nerve as much as possible. So Wolgast signaled quarterback to send the ball once more by Midshipman Dave.

Another seven yards was gained by Darrin. The West Point men were gasping, more from chagrin than from actual physical strain. Was it going to prove impossible to stop these mad Navy rushes?

Then Wolgast reluctantly as he saw Dave limp slightly, decided upon working Page and Farley a little harder just at present. So back the ball traveled to the right flank was making, however, the Navy cheermaster started a triumphant yell going, in which nearly eight hundred midshipmen joined with all their lung power.

Of course, the Army cheermaster came back with a stirring West Point yell, but one spectator, behind the side lines, turned and bawled at the Army cheermaster:

"That's right, young man! Anything on earth to keep up your crowd's courage! "

In the laugh that followed many a gray-clad cadet joined simply because he could not help himself.

"If we don't break at some point it's all ours to-day, " Wolgast was informing the players nearest him. "I've never seen Darry so wildly capable as he is right now. The demon of victory seems to have seized him. "

Dave's limp had vanished. He was ready for work—-aching for it. Wolgast worked his left flank once more, and the Army was sorely pressed.

"Brace up, Army! " was the word passing again among the West Point men. Douglass, captain of the Army team, was scolding under his breath.

But straight on Darrin and Dalzell worked the ball. It was when Wolgast decided to rest his left that Farley and Page came in for more work. These two midshipmen were excellent football men, but the Army's left was well defended. The Navy lost the ball on downs. But the Army boys were sweating, for the Navy was now within nine yards of goal line.

The Army fought it back, gaining just half a yard too little in three plays, so the ball came back to the blue and gold ranks of the Navy.

"Brace, Army! " was the word that Cadet Douglass passed. "And look out, on the right, for Darrin and Dalzell! "

There was a feint of sending the ball to Farley, but Darrin had it instead. The entire Army line, however, was alert for this very trick. Playing in sheer desperation, the cadets stopped the midshipmen when but a yard and a half had been gained. With the next play the gain was but half a yard. The third play was blocked, and once more the cadets received the pigskin.

Both Army and Navy cheermasters now refrained from inviting din. Those of the spectators who boosted for the Army were now silent, straining their vision and holding their breath. It began to look, this year, as though the Navy could do with the Army as it pleased.

Wolgast lined his men up for a fierce onslaught Darrin and Dalzell, panting, looked like a pair who would die in their tracks ere allowing the ball to go by them.

In a moment more the Army signal was being called out crisply. The whistle sounded, and both elevens were in instant action.

But the cadets failed to get through. The middies were driving them back. In sheer desperation the cadet with the ball turned and dropped behind the Army goal line—-a safety.

CHAPTER XIV

THE NAVY GOAT GRINS

All at once the Navy band chopped out a few swift measures of triumphant melody.

The entire Brigade of Midshipmen cheered under its cheermaster. Thousands of blue and gold Navy banners fluttered through the stands.

That safety had counted two on the score for the Navy.

Given breathing time, the Army now brought the ball out toward midfield, and once more the savage work began. The Navy had gained ten yards, when the time-keeper signaled the end of the first period.

As the players trotted off the Navy was exultant, the Army depressed. Captain Douglass was scowling.

"You fellows will have to brace! " he snapped. "Are you going to let the little middies run over us? "

"I shall have no bad feeling, suh, if you think it well to put a fresh man in my place, suh, " replied Cadet Anstey.

"Hang it, I don't want a man in your place! " retorted Douglass angrily. "I want you, and every other man, Anstey, to do each better work than was done in that period. Hang it, fellows, the middies are making sport of us. "

Among the Navy players there was not so much talk. All were deeply contented with events so far.

"I've no remarks to make, fellows, " Captain Wolgast remarked. "You are all playing real football. "

"At any rate Darry and his grinning twin are, " chuckled Jetson. "My, but you can see the hair rise on the Army right flank when Darry and Danny leap at them! "

In the second period, which started off amid wild yelling from the onlookers, the Army fought hard and fiercely, holding back the Navy somewhat. During the period two of the cadets were so badly hurt that the surgeons ordered them from the field. Two fresh subs. came into the eleven, and after that the Army seemed endowed with a run of better luck. The second period closed with no change in the score, though at the time of the timekeeper's interference the Navy had the ball within eleven yards of the Army goal line.

"We've got the Navy stopped, now, I think, " murmured Douglass to his West Point men. "All we've got to do now is to keep 'em stopped. "

"If they don't break our necks, or make us stop from heart failure, suh, " replied Cadet Anstey, with a grimace.

"We've got the Army tired enough. We must go after them in the third period, " announced Captain Wolgast.

But this did not happen until the third time that the Navy got the pigskin. Then Darrin and Dalzell, warned, began to run the ball down the field. Here a new feint was tried. When the Navy started in motion every Army man was sure that Wolgast was going to try to put through a center charge. It was but a ruse, however. Darrin had the pigskin, and Dalzell was boosting him through. The entire Navy line charged with the purpose of one man. There came the impact, and then the Army line went down. Darrin was charging, Dalzell and Jetson running over all who got in the way. The halfback on that side of the field was dodged. Dalzell and Jetson bore down on the victim at the same instant, and Dave, running to the side like a flash, had the ball over the line.

Wolgast himself made the kick to follow, and the score was now eight to nothing.

The applause that followed was enough to turn wiser heads. When play was resumed the Army was fighting mad. It was now victory or death for the soldier boys. The West Point men were guilty of no fouls. They played squarely and like gentlemen, but they cared nothing for snapping muscles and sinews. Before the mad work the Navy was borne back. Just before the close of the third period, the Navy was forced to make a safety on its own account.

"But Wolgast was satisfied, and the Navy coaches more than pleased.

"There's a fourth period coming, " Wolgast told himself. "But for Darry and his splendid interference the Army would get our scalp yet. Darry looks to be all right, and I believe he is. He'll hold out for the fourth. "

Eight to two, and the game three quarters finished. The Army cheermaster did his duty, but did it half dejectedly, the cadets following with rolling volumes of noise intended to mask sinking hearts. When it came the Navy's turn to yell, the midshipmen risked the safety of their windpipes. The Naval Academy Band was playing with unwonted joy.

"Fellows, nothing on earth will save us but a touchdown and a kick, " called Douglass desperately, when he got his West Point men aside. "That will tie the score. It's our best chance to-day. "

"Unless, suh, " gravely observed Anstey, "We can follow that by driving the midshipmen into a safety. "

"And we could do even that, if we had Prescott and Holmesy here, " thought Douglass, with sinking heart to himself. He was careful not to repeat that sentiment audibly.

"Holmesy ought to be here to-day, and working, " growled one of the Army subs. "He's a sneak, just to desert on Mr. Prescott's account. "

"None of that! " called Doug sharply.

The Army head coach came along, talking quietly but forcefully to the all but discouraged cadets. Then he addressed himself to Douglass, explaining what he thought were next to the weakest points in the Navy line.

"You ought to be able to save the score yet, Mr. Douglass, " wound up coach.

"I wish some one else had the job! " sighed Doug to himself.

"Fellows, the main game that is left, " explained Wolgast to the midshipmen, "is to keep West Point from scoring. As to our own points, we have enough now—-though more will be welcome. "

Play began in the fourth period. At first it was nip and tuck, neck and neck. But the Army braced and put the pigskin within sixteen yards of the Navy's goal line. Then the men from Annapolis seemed suddenly to wake up. Darrin, who had had little to do in the last few plays, was now sent to the front again. Steadily, even brilliantly, he, Dalzell and Jetson figured in the limelight plays. Yard after yard was gained, while the Army eleven shivered. At last it came to the inevitable. The Army was forced to use another safety. Stinging under the sense of defeat, the cadet players put that temporary chance to such good advantage that they gradually got the pigskin over into Naval territory. But there the midshipmen held it until the timekeeper interposed.

The fourth period and the game were over. West Point had gone down in a memorable, stinging defeat. The Navy had triumphed, ten to two.

What a crash came from the Naval Academy Band! Yet the Military Academy Band, catching the spirit and the tune, joined in, and both bands blared forth, the musicians making themselves heard faintly through all the tempest of huzzas.

Dave Darrin smiled faintly as he hurried away from the field. All his personal interest in football had vanished. He had played his last game of football and was glad that the Navy had won; that was about all.

Yet he was not listless—-far from it. On the contrary Dave fairly ran to dressing quarters, hustled under a shower and then began to towel and dress.

For out in the audience, well he knew, had sat Belle Meade and her mother.

"Darry, you're a wonder! " cried Wolgast. "Every time to-day we called upon you you were ready with the push. "

But Dave, rushing through his dressing, barely heard this and other praise that was showered on him.

"I'll get along before assembly time, Davy, " whispered Dan Dalzell.

"Come along now, " Dave called back.

"Oh, no! I know that you and Belle want some time to yourselves, " murmured Dalzell wisely. "I'll get along at the proper time. "

Dave didn't delay to argue. He stepped briskly outside, then into the field, his eyes roving over the thousands of spectators who still lingered. At last a waving little white morsel of a handkerchief rewarded Darrin's search.

"Oh, you did just splendidly to-day, " was Belle's enthusiastic greeting, as Dave stepped up to the young lady and her mother. "I've heard lots of men say that it was all Darrin's victory. "

"Yes; you're the hero of Franklin Field, this year, " smiled Mrs. Meade.

"Laura Bentley and her mother didn't come over? " Dave inquired presently.

"No; of course not——after the way that the cadets used Dick Prescott, " returned Belle. "Wasn't it shameful of the cadets to treat a man like Dick in that fashion? "

"I have my opinion, of course, " Dave replied moodily, "but it's hardly for a midshipman to criticise the cadets for their own administration of internal discipline in their own corps. The absence of Prescott and Holmes probably cost the Army the game to-day. "

"Not a bit of it! " Belle disputed warmly. "Dave, don't belittle your own superb work in that fashion! The Army would have lost to-day if the West Point eleven had been made up exclusively of Prescotts and Holmeses! "

As Belle spoke thus warmly her gaze wandered, resting, though not by intent, on the face of a young Army officer passing at that moment.

"If the remark was made to me, miss, " smiled the Army officer, "I wish to say that I wholly agree with you. The Navy's playing was the most wonderful that I ever saw. "

Dave, in the meantime, had saluted, then stood at attention until the Army officer had passed.

"There! " cried Belle triumphantly. "You have it from the other side, now—-from the enemy. "

"Hardly from the enemy, " replied Dave, laughing. "Between the United States Army and the United States Navy there can never be a matter of enmity. Annually, in football, the Army and Navy teams are opponents—-rivals, perhaps—-but never enemies. "

Mrs. Meade had strolled away for a few yards, the better to leave the young people by themselves.

"Dave, " announced Belle almost sternly, "you've simply got to say something savage about the action of the West Point men in sending Dick Prescott to Coventry. "

"The West Point men didn't do it, " rejoined Dave. "It was all done by the members of the first class alone. "

"Well, then, you must say something very disagreeable about the first class at the Military Academy. "

"But why? " persisted Dave Darrin. He was disgusted enough over the action of the first class cadets, but, being in the service himself, he felt it indelicate in him to criticise the action of the cadets of the United States Military Academy.

"Why? " repeated Belle. "Why, simply because Laura Bentley will insist on asking me when I get home what you had to say about Dick's case. If I can't tell Laura that you said something pretty nearly awful, then Laura will be terribly hurt. "

"Shall I swear? " asked Dave innocently.

Belle opened her eyes wide in amazement.

"No, you won't swear, " Belle retorted. "Profanity isn't the accomplishment of a gentleman. But you must say something about Dick's case which will show her that all of Dick's friends are standing by the poor fellow. "

"But, Belle, you know it isn't considered very manly for a fellow in one branch of the service to say anything against fellows in the other branch. "

"Not even—-for Laura's sake? "

"Oh, well, " proposed Midshipman Darrin, squirming about between the horns of the dilemma, "you just think of whatever will please Laura most to hear from me. "

"Yes——-? " pressed Miss Meade.

"Then tell it to her and say that I said it. "

"But how can I say that you said it if you didn't say it? " demanded Belle, pouting prettily.

"Easiest thing in the world, Belle. I authorize you, fully, to say whatever you like about Dick, as coming from me. If I authorize you to say it, then you won't be fibbing, will you? "

Belle had to think that over. It was a bit of a puzzle, as must be admitted.

"Now, let's talk about ourselves, " Darrin pressed her. "I see Danny boy coming, with that two-yard grin of his, and we won't have much further chance to talk about ourselves. "

The two young people, therefore, busied themselves with personal talk. Dan drifted along, but merely raised his cap to Belle, then stationed himself by Mrs. Meade's side.

It was not until Dave signaled quietly that Dalzell came over to take Belle's proffered hand and chat for a moment.

The talk was all too short for all concerned. A call of the bugle signaled the midshipmen to leave friends and hasten back for assembly.

It was not until the train had started away from Philadelphia that Dave and Dan were all but mobbed by way of congratulation. Wolgast, Jetson, Farley, Page and others also came in for their share of good words.

"And to think, Darry, that you can never play on the Navy eleven again! " groaned a second classman.

"You'll have some one else in my place, " laughed Dave.

"The Navy never before had a football player like you, and we'll never have one again, " insisted the same man. "Dalzell's kind come once in about every five years, but your kind, Darry, never come back—-in the Navy! "

CHAPTER XV

DAN FEELS AS "SOLD" AS HE LOOKS

It was the first hop after the New Year.

"Tell me one thing Dave, " begged Belle Meade, who, with Laura Bentley, and accompanied by Mrs. Meade, had come down to Annapolis for this dance.

"I'll tell you two things, if I know how, " Darrin responded promptly.

"Dan has danced a little with Laura, to be sure, but he introduced Mr. Farley to her, and has written down Farley's name for a lot of dances on Laura's card. "

"Farley is a nice fellow, " Dave replied. "But why didn't Dan want more of the dances with Laura, instead of turning them over to Mr. Farley? " followed up Belle. "And—-there he goes now. "

"Farley? "

"No, stupid! Dan. "

"Well, why shouldn't he move about? " Midshipman Darrin inquired.

"But with—-By the way, who is that girl, anyway? "

The girl was tall, rather stately and of a pronounced blonde type. She was a girl who would have been called more than merely pretty by any one who had seen her going by on Midshipman Dalzell's arm.

"I don't really know who she is, " Dave admitted.

"Have you seen her here before? "

"Yes; I think I have seen the young lady half a dozen times before to-night. "

"Then it's odd that you don't know who she is, " pursued Miss Meade.

"I've never been introduced to her, you see. "

"Oh! I imagined that you midshipmen were always being presented to girls. "

"That's a fairy tale, " said Dave promptly. "The average midshipman has about all he can do to hold his place here, without losing any time in running around making the acquaintances of young women who probably don't care at all about knowing him. "

"What I'm wondering about, " Belle went on, "is whether the young woman we have been discussing is any one in whom Dan Dalzell is seriously interested. "

"I'll ask Dan. "

"Oh! And I suppose you'll tell him that it's I who really want to know. "

"I'll tell him that, too, if you wish it. "

"Dave, you won't even mention my name to Dan in connection with any topic so silly. "

"All right, Belle. All I want is my sailing orders. I know how to follow them. "

"You're teasing me, " Miss Meade went on, pouting. "I don't mean to be curious, but I noticed that Dan appears to be quite attentive to the young lady, and I was wondering whether Dan had met his fate--that's all. "

"I don't know, " smiled Midshipman Darrin, "and I doubt if Dan does, either. He's just the kind of fellow who might ignore girls for three years, then be ardently attentive to one for three days--and forget all about her in a week. "

"Is Dan such a flirt as that? " Belle demanded, looking horrified.

"Dan—-a flirt! " chuckled Dave. "I shall have to tell that to some of the fellows; it will amuse them. No; I wouldn't call Dan a flirt. He's anything but that. Dan will either remain a bachelor until he's past forty, or else some day he'll marry suddenly after having known the girl at least twenty-four hours. Dan hasn't much judgment where girls are concerned. "

"He appears to be able to tell a pretty girl when he sees one, " argued Belle Meade, turning again to survey Dan's companion.

Belle, with the sharp eyes and keen intuition of her sex, was quite justified in believing that Midshipman Dalzell realized fully the charms of the girl with whom he was talking.

Miss Catharine Atterly was the only daughter of wealthy parents, though her father had started life as a poor boy. Daniel Atterly, however, had been shrewd enough to know the advantages of a better education than he had been able to absorb in his boyhood. Miss Catharine, therefore, had been trained in some of the most expensive, if not the best, schools in the country. She was a buxom, healthy girl, full of the joy of living, yet able to conceal her enthusiasm under the polish that she had acquired in the schools she had attended. Miss Atterly, on coming to Annapolis, had conceived a considerable liking for the Naval uniform, and had attracted Dan to her side within the last three days. And Dan had felt his heart beating faster when nearing this pretty young creature.

Now, he was endeavoring to display himself to the best advantage before her eyes.

"You midshipmen have a very graceful knack of being charmingly attentive to the ladies, " Miss Atterly suggested coyly.

"We receive a little bit of training in social performance, if that is what you mean, Miss Atterly, " Dan replied.

"And that enables you to be most delightfully attentive to every girl that comes along? "

"I don't know, " Midshipman Dalzell replied slowly. "I haven't had much experience. "

Miss Atterly laughed as though she felt certain that she knew better.

"Do you say that to every girl? " she asked.

"I don't get many chances, " Dan insisted. "Miss Atterly, all the hops that I've attended could be counted on your fingers, without using the thumbs? "

"Oh, really? "

"It is the truth, I assure you. Some of the midshipmen attend many hops. Most of us are too busy over our studies as a rule. "

"Then you prefer books to the society of girls? "

"It isn't that, " replied Dan, growing somewhat red under Miss Atterly's amused scrutiny. "The fact is that a fellow comes here to the Naval Academy for the purpose of becoming an officer in the Navy. "

"To be sure. "

"And, unless the average fellow hugs his books tightly he doesn't have any show to get through and become an officer. There are some fellows, of course, to whom the studies come easily. With most of us it's a terrible grind. Even with the grind about forty per cent. of the fellows who enter the Naval Academy are found deficient and are dropped. If you are interested in knowing, I had a fearful time in keeping up with the requirements. "

"Oh, you poor boy! " cried Miss Atterly half tenderly.

"I never felt that I wanted any sympathy, " Dan declared stoutly. "If I couldn't keep up, then the only thing to do was to go back to civil life and find my own level among my own kind. "

"Now, that was truly brave in you! " declared Miss Atterly, admiration shining in her eyes.

"There's the music starting, " Dan hastily reminded her. "Our dance. "

"Would it seem disagreeable in me if I asked you to sit out this number with me? " inquired the girl. "The truth is, I can dance any evening, but you and your brave fight here, Mr. Dalzell, interest me—-oh, more than I can tell you! "

Under this line of conversation Midshipman Dalzell soon began to feel highly uncomfortable. Miss Atterly, however, in getting Dan to talk of the midshipman and the Naval life, soon had him feeling at his ease. Nor could Dalzell escape noticing the fact that Miss Atterly appeared to enjoy his company hugely.

Then Dan was led on into talking of the life of the Naval officer at sea, and he spoke eloquently.

"A life of bravery and daring, " commented Miss Atterly thoughtfully. "Yet, after all, I would call it rather a lonely life. "

"Perhaps it will prove so, " Dalzell assented. "Yet it is all the life that I look forward to. It's all the life that I care about. "

"Despite the loneliness—-or rather, because of it—-it will seem all the finer and more beautiful to come home to wife and children, " said Miss Atterly after a pause. "Nearly all Naval officers marry, don't they? "

"I—-I believe they do, " Dalzell stammered. "I—-I never asked any Naval officers for statistics. "

"Now, you are becoming droll, " cried Miss Atterly, her laughter ringing out.

"I didn't mean to be, " Dan protested. "I beg your pardon. "

Whereat Miss Atterly laughed more than ever.

"I like you even better when you're droll, " Miss Atterly informed him.

Something in the way that she said it pleased Midshipman Dalzell so immensely that he began to notice, more than before, what a very fine girl Miss Atterly was. Then, to win her applause, Dan made the mistake of trying to be funny, whereat the girl was extremely kind.

"Dave, " whispered Belle soon after the music had stopped, "I can't get away from the belief that Dan's companion is leading him on. See! Dan now looks at her almost adoringly. "

Laura Bentley, too, had noticed Dan's preoccupation, but she merely smiled within herself. She did not believe that Dan could really be serious where girls were concerned. Now, as Laura's midshipman partner led her to a seat, and soon left her, Dan, tearing himself away from Miss Atterly, came to remind Laura that his name was written on her card for the next dance.

"Very fine girl I've been talking with, Laura, " Dan confided in the straightforward way that he had always used with Miss Bentley, who was such a very old school friend.

"She certainly is very pretty, " Laura nodded.

"And—-er—-distinguished looking, don't you think? " Dan ventured.

"Yes, indeed. "

"But I was speaking more of her character—-at least, her disposition. Miss Atterly is highly sympathetic. I wish you'd meet her, Laura. "

"I shall be delighted to do so, Dan. "

"After this dance, then? And I want Belle to meet her, too. Miss Atterly has noticed you both, and was much interested when she learned that you were old school-day friends of mine. "

So, after the music had ceased, Dan escorted Laura over to where Dave and Belle were chatting.

"Belle, " asked Dan in his most direct way, "will you come and be introduced to Miss Atterly? "

"The young lady you've been dancing with so much? " Miss Meade inquired. "The tall, stately blonde? "

"Yes, " Dan nodded.

"I shall be glad to meet Miss Atterly. But how about her? Do you think she could stand the shock? "

"Miss Atterly is very anxious to meet you both, " Dalzell assured Belle.

"Take me over and shock her, then, " laughed Belle.

Dan stood gazing about the scene. "I—-I wonder where Miss Atterly is? " Dan mused aloud.

"Oh, I can tell you, " Belle answered. "A moment ago she went through the entrance over yonder. "

"Alone? "

"No; an older woman, probably Miss Atterly's mother, was with her. "

"Oh! Let's look them up, then, if you don't mind. "

As Belle rose, taking Dave's arm, Dan and Laura took the lead.

Just beyond the entrance that Belle had indicated no one else was in sight when the four young friends reached the spot. There was a clump of potted tropical shrubbery at one side.

On the other side of this shrubbery sat Mrs. and Miss Atterly, engaged in conversation.

"Why do you prefer to sit in this out-of-the-way place, Catharine? " her mother inquired, just as the young people came up.

"I want to get away from two rather goodlooking but very ordinary girls that Mr. Dalzell wants to present to me, mamma, " she replied.

"If they are midshipmen's friends are they too ordinary to know? " inquired Mrs. Atterly.

"Mamma, if I am going to interest Mr. Dalzell, I don't want other girls stepping in at every other moment. I don't want to know his girl friends. "

"Are you attracted to Mr. Dalzell, Cathy? " asked her mother.

"Not especially, I assure you, mamma. "

"Oh, then it is not a serious affair. "

"It may be, " laughed the girl lightly. "If I can learn to endure Mr. Dalzell, then I may permit him to marry me when he is two years older and has his commission. "

"Even if you don't care much for him? " asked Mrs. Atterly, almost shocked.

"If I marry, " pouted Miss Atterly, "I don't want a husband that leaves the house every morning, and returns every evening. "

"Cathy! "

"Well, I don't! In some ways I suppose it's nice to be a married woman. One has more freedom in going about alone. Now, a Naval officer, mamma, would make the right sort of husband for me. He'd be away, much of the time, on long cruises. "

"But I understand, Cathy, that sometimes a Naval officer has a year or two of shore duty. "

"If that happened, " laughed the girl, "I could take a trip to Europe couldn't I? And the social position of a Naval officer isn't a bad one. His wife enjoys the same social position, you know, mamma. "

"Yet why Mr. Dalzell, if you really don't care anything about him? "

"Because he's so simple, mamma. He would be dreadfully easy to manage! "

The four young people looking for the Atterlys had unavoidably heard every word. They halted, Dan violently red in the face. Then Laura, with quick tact, wheeled about and led the way back to the ball room floor.

"Better luck next time, Dan, " whispered Belle, gripping Dalzell's arm.

"Don't you think twice is enough for a simpleton like me? " blurted Midshipman Dan.

CHAPTER XVI

THE DAY OF MANY DOUBTS

Busy days followed, days which, for some of the first classmen, were filled with a curious discontent.

Some, to be sure, among these midshipmen soon to graduate, took each day as it came, with little or no emotion. To them the Naval life ahead was coming only as a matter of course. There were others, however—-and Dave Darrin was among them—-who looked upon a commission as an officer of the Navy as a sacred trust given them by the nation.

Dave Darrin was one of those who, while standing above the middle of his class, yet felt that he had not made sufficiently good use of his time. To his way of thinking there was an appalling lot in the way of Naval duties that he did not understand.

"I may get through here, and out of here, and in another couple of years be a line or engineer officer, " Midshipman Darrin confided to his chum and roommate one day. "But I shall be only a half-baked sort of officer. "

"Well, are cubs ever anything more? " demanded Dan.

"Yes; Wolgast, for instance, is going to be something more. So will Fenton and Day, and several others whom I could name. "

"And so is Darrin, " confidently predicted Midshipman Dalzell.

But Dave shook his head.

"No, no, Danny boy. The time was when I might have believed extremely well of myself, but that day has gone by. When I entered the Naval Academy I probably thought pretty well of myself. I've tried to keep up with the pace here—-—-"

"And you've done it, and are going to do it right along, " interjected Midshipman Dalzell.

"No; it almost scares me when I look over the subjects that I'm not really fit in. It's spring, now, and I'm only a few weeks away from graduation, only something like two years this side of a commission as ensign, and—-and—-Dan, I wonder if I'm honestly fit to command a rowboat."

"You've got a brief grouch against yourself, Davy," muttered Dan.

"No; but I think I know what a Naval officer should be, and I also know how far short I fall of what I should be."

"If you get your diploma," argued Midshipman Dalzell, "the faculty of the Naval Academy will testify on the face of it that you're a competent midshipman and on your way to being fit to hold an ensign's commission presently."

"But that's just the point, Danny. I shall know, myself, that I'm only a poor, dub sort of Naval officer. I tell you, Danny, I don't know enough to be a good Naval officer."

"Then that's a reflection on your senior officers who have had your training on hand," grinned Dalzell. "If you talk in the same vein after you've gotten your diploma, it will amount to a criticism of the intelligence of your superior officers. And that's something that's wisely forbidden by the regulations."

Dan picked up a text-book and opened it, as though he believed that he had triumphantly closed the discussion. Midshipman Darrin, however, was not to be so easily silenced.

"Then, if you're not fitted to be a Naval officer," blurted Dalzell, "what on earth can be said of me?"

"You may not stand quite as high as I do, on mere markings," Dave assented. "But there are a lot of things, Danny, that you know much better than I do."

"Name one of them," challenged Dalzell.

"Well, steam engineering, for instance. Now, I'm marked higher in that than you are, Danny. Yet, when the engine on one of the steamers goes wrong you can hunt around until you get the engine to running smoothly. You're twice as clever at that as I am."

"Not all Naval officers are intended to be engineer officers, " grunted Midshipman Dalzell. "If you don't feel clever enough in that line, just put in your application for watch officer's work. "

"Take navigation, " Dave continued. "I stand just fairly well in the theory of the thing. But I've no real knack with a sextant. "

"Well, the sextant is only a hog-yoke, " growled Dalzell.

"Yes; but I shiver every time I pick up the hog-yoke under the watchful gaze of an instructor. "

"Humph! Only yesterday I heard Lieutenant-Commander Richards compliment you for your work in nav. "

"Yes; but that was the mathematical end. I'm all right on the paper end and the theoretical work, but it's the practical end that I'm afraid of. "

"You'll get plenty of the practical work as soon as you graduate and get to sea, " Dan urged.

"Yes; and very likely make a chump of myself, like Digby, of last year's class. Did you hear what he did in nav.? "

"No, " replied Dalzell, looking up with real interest this times "If Digby made a fool of himself I'll be glad to hear about it, for Dig was always just a little bit too chesty to suit me. "

"Well, Dig wasn't a bit chesty the first day that he was ordered to shoot the sun, " Dave laughed. "Dig took the sextant, and made a prize shot, or thought he did. After he had got the sun, plumb at noon, he lowered the instrument and made his reading most carefully. Then he went into the chart room, and got busy with his calculations. The longer Dig worked the worse his head ached. He stared at his figures, tore them up and tried again. Six or eight times he worked the problem over, but always with the same result. The navigating officer, who had worked the thing out in two minutes, sat back in his chair and looked bored. You see, Dig's own eyes had told him that the ship was working north, and about five miles off the coast of New Jersey. But his figures told him that the ship was anchored in the old fourth ward of the city of Newark. Try as he would, Dig couldn't get the battleship away from that ward. "

Dan Dalzell leaned back, laughing uproariously at the mental picture that this story of Midshipman Digby brought up in his mind.

"It sounds funny, when you hear it, " Dave went on. "But I sometimes shiver over the almost certainty that I'm going to do something just as bad when I get to sea. If I get sent to the engine room I'll be likely to fill the furnaces with water and the boilers with coal. "

"Rot! " objected Dan. "You're not crazy—-not even weak-minded. "

"Or else, if I'm put to navigating, I'm fairly likely to bring the battleship into violent collision with the Chicago Limited, over in Ohio. "

"Come out of that funk, Davy! " ordered his chum.

"I'm trying to, Danny boy; but there's many an hour when I feel that I haven't learned here all that I should have learned, and that I'll be miles behind the newest ensigns and lieutenants. "

"There's just about one thing for you to do, then, " proposed Dan.

"Resign? " queried Darrin, looking quizzically at his chum.

"Not by a long sight. Just go in for a commission as second lieutenant of marines. You can get that and hold it. A marine officer doesn't have to know anything but the manual of arms and a few other little simple things. "

"But a marine officer isn't a real sailor, Danny. He lives and works on a warship, to be sure, but he's more of a soldier. Now, as it happens, my whole heart and soul are wrapped up in being a Naval officer—-a real Naval officer. "

"With that longing, and an Annapolis diploma, " teased Dalzell, "there is just one thing to do. "

"What? "

"Beat your way to the realization of your dream. You've got a thundering good start. "

Midshipman Dave Darrin was not the kind to communicate his occasional doubts to anyone except his roommate. Had Darrin talked on the subject with other members of his class he would have found that many of his classmates were tortured by the same doubts that assailed him. With midshipmen who were destined to get their diplomas such doubts were to be charged only to modesty, and were therefore to their credit. Yet, every spring dozens of Annapolis first classmen are miserable, instead of feeling the joyous appeal of the budding season. They are assailed by just such fears as had reached Dave Darrin.

Dalzell, on the other hand, was tortured by no such dreads. He went hammering away with marvelous industry, and felt sure, in his own mind, that he would be retired, in his sixties, an honored rear admiral.

Had there been only book studies some of the first classmen would have broken down under the nervous strain. However, there was much to be done in the shops—-hard, physical labor, that had to be performed in dungaree clothing; toil of the kind that plastered the hard-worked midshipmen with grime and soot. There were drills, parades, cross-country marches. The day's work at the Naval Academy, at any season of the year, is arranged so that hard mental work is always followed by lively physical exertion, much of it in the open air.

Dalzell, returning one afternoon from the library encountered Midshipman Farley, who was looking unaccountably gloomy.

"What's the trouble, Farl—-dyspepsia? " grinned Dan, linking one arm through his friend's. "Own up! "

"Danny, I'm in the dumps, " confessed Farley. "I hate to acknowledge it, but I've been fearfully tempted, for the last three days, to send in my resignation. "

"What's her name? " grinningly demanded Dalzell, who had bravely recovered from his own two meetings with Venus.

"It isn't a girl—-bosh! " jeered Farley. "There's only one girl in the world I'm interested in—-and she's my kid sister. "

"Then why this talk of resigning. "

"Danny, I'm simply afraid that I'm not made of the stuff to make a competent Naval officer. My markings are all right, but I know that I don't know enough to take a sailboat out and bring it back. "

"Oh, is that all? " cried Dalzell laughingly. "Then I know just what you want. "

"What? "

"Drop into our room and have a talk with Darry. Dave knows just how to comfort and cheer a fellow who has that glum bug in his head of cabbage. Come right along! "

Dan almost forced Farley to the door of the room, opened it and shoved the modest midshipman inside.

"Darry, " Dan called joyously, "here's a case for your best talents. Farley has a pet bee in his bonnet that he isn't fit to be a Naval officer. He doesn't know enough. So he's going to resign. I've told him you'll know just how to handle his case. Go after him, now! "

Midshipman Dalzell pulled the door shut, chuckling softly to himself, and marched back to the library. It was just before the call for supper formation when Dan returned from "boning" in the library.

"Did you brace Farl up, Davy? " demanded Dan.

"You grinning idiot! " laughed Darrin. "What on earth made you bring him to me? "

"Because I thought you needed each other. "

"Well, perhaps we did, " laughed Midshipman Darrin. "At any rate I've been hammering at Farl all the time that he wasn't hammering at me. I certainly feel better, and I hope that he does. "

"You both needed the same thing, " declared Dan, grinning even more broadly as he picked up his hair brushes.

"What did we need? "

"You've both been studying so hard that your brain cells are clogged."

"But what did Farley and I both need?" insisted Midshipman Darrin.

"Mental exercise—-brain-sparring," rejoined Dalzell. "You both needed something that could take you out of the horrible daily grooves that you've been sailing in lately. You both needed something to stir you up—-and I hope you gave each other all the excitement you could."

In the way of a stirring-up something was about to happen that was going to stir up the whole first class—-if not the entire brigade.

Nor was Dave Darrin to escape being one of the central figures in the excitement.

Here is the way in which the whole big buzzing-match got its start and went on to a lively finish.

CHAPTER XVII

MR. CLAIRY DEALS IN OUTRAGES

"Mr. Darrin! "

With that hail proceeded sharply from the lips of a first classman, who on this evening happened to be the midshipman in charge of the floor.

Clairy sat at his desk in the corridor, his eyes on a novel until Dave happened along. As he gave the sharp hail Mr. Clairy thrust his novel under a little pile of text-books.

"Well, sir? " inquired Dave, halting. "Mr. Darrin, what do you mean by coming down the corridor with both shoes unlaced. "

"They are not unlaced, " retorted Dave, staring in amazement at Midshipman Clairy.

"They are not now—-true. "

"And they haven't been unlaced, sir, since I first laced them on rising this morning. "

"Don't toy with the truth, Mr. Darrin! " rang Clairy's voice sternly.

"If my shoes had been unlaced, they would still be unlaced, wouldn't they, sir? " demanded Dave.

"No; for you have laced them since I spoke to you about it! "

This was entirely too much for Darrin, who gulped, gasped, and then stared again at the midshipman in charge of the floor.

Then, suddenly, a light dawned on Dave. He grinned almost as broadly as Dan Dalzell could have done.

"Come, come, now, Clairy! " chided Dave. "What on earth is the joke—-and why? "

Midshipman Clairy straightened himself, his eyes flashing and his whole appearance one of intense dignity.

"Mr. Darrin, there is no joke about it, as you are certainly aware, sir. And I must call your attention to the fact that it is bad taste to address a midshipman familiarly when he is on official duty. "

"Why, hang you—-" Dave broke forth utterly aghast.

"Stop, sir! " commanded Mr. Clairy, rising. "Mr. Darrin, you will place yourself on report for strolling along the corridor with both shoes unlaced. You will also place yourself on report for impertinence in answering the midshipman in charge of the floor. "

"But——-"

"Go at once, sir, and place yourself on report"

Dave meditated, for two or three seconds, over the advisability of knocking Mr. Clairy down. But familiarity with the military discipline of the Naval Academy immediately showed Darrin that his only present course was to obey.

"I wonder who's loony now? " hummed Dave to himself, as he marched briskly along on his way to the office of the officer in charge. There be picked up two of the report slips, dipping a pen in ink.

First, in writing, he reported himself on the charge of having his shoes unlaced. In the space for remarks Darrin wrote tersely:

"Untrue. "

Against the charge of unwarranted impertinence to the midshipman in charge of the floor Dave wrote the words:

"Impertinence admitted, but in my opinion entirely warranted. "

So utterly astounded was Darrin by this queer turn of affairs, that he forgot the matter that had taken him from his room. On his way back he met Midshipman Page. On the latter's face was a look as black as a thundercloud.

"What on earth is wrong, Page? " Darrin asked.

"I've got the material for a first-class fight on my hands, " Page answered, his eyes flashing.

"What—-"

"Clairy has ordered me to report myself. "

"What does he say you were doing that you weren't doing? " inquired Midshipman Darrin, a curious look in his eyes.

"Clairy has the nerve to state that I was coming along the corridor with my blouse unbuttoned. He ordered me to button it up, which I couldn't do since it was already buttoned. But he declared that I buttoned it up while facing him, and so I'm on my way to place myself on report for an offense that I didn't commit. "

"Clairy just sent me to the O. C. to frap the pap for having my shoes unlaced, " remarked Dave, his face flushing darkly.

"What on earth is Clairy up to? " cried Page.

"I don't know. I can't see his game clearly. But he's certainly hunting trouble. "

"Then——-"

"See here, Page, we've no business holding indignation meetings in study hours. But come to my room just as soon as release sounds—-will you? "

"You can wager that I will, " shot back Midshipman Page as he started along the corridor.

"Hello, " hailed Midshipman Dalzell, looking up as his chum entered. "Why, Darry, you're angry—-really angry. Who has dared throw spitballs at you? "

"Quit your joking, Dan! " returned Dave Darrin, his voice quivering. "Clairy is hunting real trouble, I imagine, and I fancy he'll have to be obliged. "

Dave thereupon related swiftly what had happened, Dan staring in sheer amazement. Then Dalzell jumped up.

"Where are you going? " Darrin answered.

"To interview Clairy. "

"You'd better not, Dan. The trouble is thick enough already. "

"I'm going to interview Clairy—-perhaps, " retorted Midshipman Dalzell. "I've just thought of a perfectly good excuse for being briefly out of quarters during study hours. I'll be back soon—-perhaps with some news. "

Off Dan posted. In less than ten minutes he returned, looking even more indignant than had his chum.

"Davy, " broke forth Dalzell hotly, "that idiot is surely hunting all the trouble there is in Annapolis. "

"He went after you, then? "

"I was making believe to march straight by the fellow's desk, " resumed Dan, "when Clairy brought me up sharply. Told me to frap the pap for strolling with my hands in my pockets. I didn't do anything like that. "

In another hour indignation was running riot in that division. Midshipman Clairy had ordered no less than eight first classmen to put themselves on report for offenses that none of them would admit having committed.

Oh, but there was wrath boiling in the quarters occupied by those eight first classmen.

Immediately after release had sounded, Page and Farley made a bee-line for Dave's room.

"Did Clairy wet you, Farley? " demanded Darrin.

"No; I haven't been out of my room until just now. "

"Page, " continued Darrin, "circulate rapidly in first class rooms on this deck and find out whether Clairy improperly held up any more of the fellows. Dan was a victim, too. "

Page had five first classmen on the scene in a few minutes. The meeting seemed doomed to resolve itself into a turmoil of angry language.

"Clairy is a hound! "

"A liar in my case! "

"He's hunting a fight! "

"Coventry would do him more good. "

"Yes; we'll have to call the class to deal with this. "

"The scoundrel! "

"The pup! "

"He's trying to pile some of us up with so many demerits that we won't be able to graduate. "

"Oh, well, " argued Page, "Fenwick has hit it. We can't fight such a lying hound. All we can do is to get the class out and send the fellow to Coventry. "

"What do you imagine it all means, Darry? " questioned Fenwick.

Dave's wrath had had time to simmer down, and he was cooler now.

"I wish I knew what to think, fellows, " Dave answered slowly. "Clairy has never shown signs of doing such things before. "

"He has always been a sulk, and never had a real friend in the class, " broke in Farley.

"He has always been quiet and reticent, " Dave admitted. "But we never before had any real grievance against Mr. Clairy. "

"We have a grievance now, all right! " glowered Page. "Coventry, swift and tight, is the only answer to the situation. "

"Let's not be in too much haste, fellows, " Darrin urged.

"You—-you give such advice as that? " gasped Midshipman Dalzell. "Why, Davy, the fellow went for you in fearful shape. He insulted you outrageously. "

"I know he did, " Darrin responded. "That's why I believe in going slowly in the matter. "

"Now, why? " hissed Page. "Why on earth—-why? "

"Clairy must have had some motive behind his attack, " Dave urged.

"It couldn't have been a good motive, anyway, " broke in another midshipman hotly.

"Never mind that part of it, just now, " Dave Darrin retorted. "Fellows, I, for one, don't like to go after Mr. Clairy too hastily while we're all in doubt about the cause of it. "

"We don't need to know the cause, " stormed indignant Farley. "We know the results, and that's enough for us. I favor calling a class meeting to-morrow night. "

"We can do just as much, and act just as intelligently, if we hold the class-meeting off for two or three nights, " Midshipman Darrin maintained.

"Now, why on earth should we bold off that long? " insisted Fenwick. "We know, now, that Mr. Clairy has insulted eight members of our class. We know that he has lied about them, and that the case is so bad as to require instant attention. All I'm sorry for is that it's too late to hold the class meeting within the next five minutes. "

Dave found even his own roommate opposed to delay in dealing with the preposterous case of the outrageous Mr. Clairy.

Yet such was Darrin's ascendency over his classmates in matters of ethics and policy, that he was able, before taps, to bring the rest around to his wish for a waiting programme for two or three days.

"There'll be some explanation of this, " Dave urged, when he had gotten his comrades into a somewhat more reasonable frame of mind.

"The explanation will have to be sought with fists, " grumbled Fenwick. "And there are eight of us, while Clairy has only two eyes that can be blackened. "

The news had spread, of course, and the first class was in a fury of resentment against one of its own members.

Meanwhile Midshipman Clairy sat at his desk out in the corridor, clearly calm and indifferent to all the turmoil that his acts had stirred up in the brigade.

CHAPTER XVIII

THE WHOLE CLASS TAKES A HAND

"Then, Mr. Darrin, you admit the use of impertinent language to Mr. Clairy, when the midshipman was in charge of the floor? "

This question was put to Dave, the following morning, by the commandant of midshipmen.

"It would have been an impertinence, sir, under ordinary conditions, " Darrin answered. "Under the circumstances I believed, sir, that I had been provoked into righteous anger. "

"You still assert that Mr. Clairy's charge that your shoes were unlaced when you approached him was false? "

"Absolutely false, sir. "

"Do you wish any time to reflect over that answer, Mr. Darrin? "

"No, sir. "

"You are willing your answer should go on record, then? "

"My denial of the charge of having my shoes unlaced is the only answer that I can possibly make, sir. "

The commandant reflected. Then he directed that Midshipman Clairy be ordered to report to him. Clairy came, almost immediately. The commandant questioned him closely. Clairy still stuck resolutely to his story that Dave Darrin had been passing through the corridor with his shoes unlaced; and, furthermore, that Darrin, when rebuked and ordered to place himself on report, had used impertinent language.

During this examination the midshipmen did not glance toward each other. Both stood at attention, their glances on the commandant's face.

"I do not know what to say, " the officer admitted at last. "I will take the matter under advisement. You may both go. "

Outside, well away from the office, Dave Darrin halted, swinging and confronting Clairy sternly.

"You lying scoundrel! " vibrated Darrin, his voice shaking with anger.

"It constitutes another offense, Mr. Darrin, to use such language for the purpose of intimidating a midshipman in the performance of his duty, " returned Midshipman Clairy, looking back steadily into Dave's eyes.

"An offense? Fighting is another, under a strict interpretation of the rules, " Dave replied coldly.

"And I do not intend to fight you, " replied Clairy, still speaking smoothly.

"Perhaps I should know better than to challenge you, " replied Midshipman Darrin. "The spirit of the brigade prohibits my fighting any one who is not a gentleman. "

"If that is all you have to say, Mr. Darrin, I will leave you. You cannot provoke me into any breach of the regulations. "

Clairy walked away calmly, leaving Dave Darrin fuming with anger.

Page was sent for next, then Dalzell. Both denied utterly the charges on which Clairy had ordered them to report themselves. Again Mr. Clairy was sent for, and once more he asserted the complete truthfulness of his charges.

It was so in the cases of the five remaining midshipmen under charges, though still Mr. Clairy stuck to the correctness of the report.

Action in all of the eight cases was suspended by the commandant, who went post-haste to the superintendent. That latter official, experienced as he was in the ways of midshipmen, could offer no solution of the mystery.

"You see, my dear Graves, " explained the superintendent, "it is the rule of custom here, and a safe rule at that, to accept the word of a midshipman as being his best recollection or knowledge of the truth of any statement that he makes. In that case, we would seem to be bound to accept the statements of Mr. Clairy. "

On the other hand, we are faced with the fact that we must accept the statements made by Mr. Darrin, Mr. Page, Mr. Dalzell, Mr. Fenwick and others. We are on the horns of a dilemma, though I doubt not that we shall find a way out of it. "

"There appears, sir, to be only the statement of one midshipman against the word of eight midshipmen, " suggested the commandant.

"Not exactly that, " replied the superintendent. "The fact is that Mr. Clairy's charges do not concern the eight midshipmen collectively, but individually. Had Mr. Clairy charged all eight of the midshipmen of an offense committed at the same time and together, and had the eight midshipmen all denied it, then we should be reluctantly compelled to admit the probability that Mr. Clairy had been lying. But his charges relate to eight different delinquencies, and not one of the eight accused midshipmen is in a position to act as witness for any of the other accused men. "

"Then what are we going to do, sir? ".

"I will admit that I do not yet know, " replied the superintendent. "Some method of getting at the truth in the matter is likely to occur to us later on. In the meantime, Graves, you will not publish any punishments for the reported delinquencies. "

"Very good, sir, " nodded the commandant.

"Keep your wits at work for a solution of the mystery, Graves. "

"I will, sir. "

"And I will give the matter all the attention that I can, " was the superintendent's last word.

If anger had been at the boiling point before, the situation was even worse now.

Page and Fenwick openly challenged Clairy to fight. He replied, in each case, with a cool, smiling refusal.

"We've got to hold that class meeting! " growled Farley.

"Why? " inquired Dave. "The class can't do anything more to Clairy than has already been done. His refusals to fight will send him to Coventry as securely as could action by all four of the classes. No fellow here can refuse to fight, unless he couples with his refusal an offer to submit the case to his own class for action. No one, henceforth, will have a word to say to Clairy. "

"Perhaps not; but I still insist that the class meeting ought to be called. "

This was the general sentiment among the first classmen. Darrin was the only real dissenter to the plan.

"Oh, well, go ahead and call the class together, if you like, " agreed Dave. "My main contention is that such a meeting will be superfluous. The action of the class has really been taken already. "

"Will you come to the meeting, Darry? " asked Fenwick.

"Really, I don't know, " Dave answered thoughtfully. "My presence would do neither good nor harm. The action of the class has already been decided. In fact, it has been put into effect. "

"Then you won't be there? " spoke up Farley.

"I don't know. I'll come, however, if it will please any of you especially. "

"Oh, bother you, Darry! We're not going to beg your presence as a favor. "

At formation for dinner, when the brigade adjutant published the orders, every midshipman in the long ranks of the twelve companies waited eagerly to learn what had been done in the cases of the eight midshipmen. They were doomed to disappointment, however.

At brigade formation for supper notice of a meeting of the first class in Recreation Hall was duly published. There was rather an unwonted hush over the tables that night.

Immediately afterwards groups of midshipmen were seen strolling through the broad foyer of Bancroft Hall, and up the low steps into Recreation Hall. Yet it was some ten minutes before there was anything like a full gathering of the first class.

"Order! " rapped the class president Then, after glancing around:

"Is Mr. Clairy present? "

He was not.

"Where's Darry? " buzzed several voices.

But Dave Darrin was not present either.

"Where is he? " several demanded of Dan.

"Blessed if I know, " Dan answered. "I wish I did, fellows. "

"Isn't Darry going to attend? "

"I don't know that, either. "

Midshipman Gosman now claimed the floor. He spoke a good deal as though he had been retained as advocate for the eight accused midshipmen. In a fiery speech Mr. Gosman recited that eight different members of the class had been falsely accused by Mr. Clairy.

"There are not eight liars in our class, " declared Midshipman Gosman, with very telling effect.

Then, after more fiery words aimed at Clairy, Mr. Gosman demanded:

"Why is not Mr. Clairy here to speak for himself? Let him who can answer this! Further, Mr. Clairy has been challenged to fight by some of those whom be accused. Now, sir and classmates, a midshipman may refuse to fight, but if he does he must submit his case to his class, and then be guided by the class decision as to whether he must fight or not. Mr. Clairy has not done this. "

"He's a cur! " shouted a voice.

"I accept the remark, " bowed Mr. Gosman, "if I am permitted to express the class's apology to all dogs for the comparison. "

"Good! " yelled several.

"Mr. President and classmates, " continued the angry orator, "I believe we are all of one mind, and I believe that I can express the unanimous sentiment of the first class. "

"You can! "

"You bet you can! "

"Go ahead! "

"Mr. President, I take it upon myself to move that the first class should, and hereby does, send Mr. Clairy to Coventry for all time to come! "

"Second the motion! " cried several voices.

Then a diversion was created.

One of the big doors opened and a midshipman stepped into the room, closing the door.

That midshipman was Dave Darrin. Every first classman in the room felt certain that Darrin had entered for the express purpose of saying something of consequence.

CHAPTER XIX

MIDSHIPMAN DARRIN HAS THE FLOOR

But Dave did not speak at first. Advancing only a short distance into the hall he stood with arms folded, his face well-nigh expressionless.

For a moment the class president glanced at Darrin, then at the assemblage.

"Gentlemen, " announced the class president, "you have heard the motion, that Mr. Clairy be sent to Coventry for all time to come. The motion has been duly seconded. Remarks are in order. "

"Mr. President! "

It was Dave who had spoken. All eyes were turned in his direction at once.

"Mr. Darrin, " announced the chair. "Mr. President, and classmates, I, for one, shall vote against the motion. "

An angry clamor rose, followed by calls of, "Question! Put the motion! "

"Do any of you know, " Darrin continued, "why Mr. Clairy is not here this evening? "

"He's afraid to come! "

"Did any of you note that Mr. Clairy was not at supper? "

"The hound hadn't any appetite, " jeered Fenwick angrily.

"You have observed, of course, that Mr. Clairy was not here at the meeting? "

"He didn't dare come! " cried several voices.

"If you have any explanation to make, Mr. Darrin, let us have it, " urged the chair.

"Mr. President and classmates, " Midshipman Darrin continued, "all along I have felt that there must be some explanation to match Mr. Clairy's most extraordinary conduct. I now offer you the explanation. The officer in charge sent for me, to impart some information that I am requested to repeat before this meeting. "

"Go on! " cried several curious voices when Dave paused for a moment.

"Fellows, I hate to tell you the news, and you will all be extremely sorry to hear it. You will be glad, however, that you did not pass the motion now before the class. Mr. President, I have to report, at the request of the officer in charge, the facts in Mr. Clairy's case.

"From the peculiar nature of the case both the superintendent and the commandant of midshipmen were convinced that there was something radically wrong with Mr. Clairy. "

"Humph! I should say so! " uttered Penwick, with emphasis.

"Mr. Clairy was not at our mess at supper, " resumed Dave Darrin, "for the very simple reason that he had been taken to hospital. There he was examined by three surgeons, assisted by an outside specialist. Mr. President and classmates, I know you will all feel heartily sorry for Clairy when I inform you that he has been pronounced insane. "

Dave ceased speaking, and an awed silence prevailed. It was the chair who first recovered his poise.

"Clairy insane! " cried the class president. "Gentlemen, now we comprehend what, before, it was impossible to understand. "

In the face of this sudden blow to a classmate all the midshipmen sat for a few minutes more as if stunned. Then they began to glance about at each other.

"I think this event must convince us, sir, " Darrin's voice broke in, "that we young men don't know everything, and that we should learn to wait for facts before we judge swiftly. "

"Mr. President! "

It was Gosman, on his feet. In a husky voice that midshipman begged the consent of his seconders for his withdrawing the motion he had offered sending Midshipman Clairy to Coventry. In a twinkling that motion had been withdrawn.

"Will Mr. Darrin, state, if able, how serious Clairy's insanity is believed to be? " inquired the chair.

"It is serious enough to ruin all his chances in the Navy, " Dave answered, "though the surgeons believe that, after Clairy has been taken by his friends to some asylum, his cure can eventually be brought about. "

The feeling in the room was too heavy for more discussion. A motion to adjourn was offered and carried, after which the first classmen hurried from the room.

Of course no demerits were imposed as a result of the crazy reports ordered by Midshipman Clairy on that memorable night. Three days later the unfortunate young man's father arrived and had his son conveyed from Annapolis. It may interest the reader to know that, two years later, the ex-midshipman fully recovered his reason, and is now successfully engaged in business.

Spring now rapidly turned into early summer. The baseball squad had been at work for some time. Both Darrin and Dalzell had been urged to join.

"Let's go into the nine, if we can make it—-and we ought to, " urged Dan.

"You go ahead, Danny boy, if you're so inclined, " replied Dave.

"Aren't you going in? "

"I have decided not to. "

"You're a great patriot for the Naval Academy, Davy. "

"I'm looking out for myself, I'll admit. I want to graduate as high in my class as I can, Danny. Yet I'd sacrifice my own desires if the Naval Academy needed me on the nine. However, I'm not needed.

There are several men on the nine who play ball better than I but don't let me keep you off the nine, Dan. "

"If you stay off I guess I will, " replied Dalzell. "If the nine doesn't need you then it doesn't need me. "

"But I thought you wanted to play. "

"Not unless you and I could be the battery, David, little giant. I'd like to catch your pitching, but I don't want to stop any other fellow's pitching. "

So far the nine had gone on without them. Realizing how much Dan wanted to play with the Navy team in this, their last year, Dave changed his mind, and both joined. A very creditable showing was made after their entrance into the nine. That year the Navy captured more than half the games played, though the Navy was fated to lose to the Army by a score of four to three. This game is described in detail in *"Dick Prescott's Fourth Year At West Point. "*

With the approach of graduation time Dave's heart was gladdened by the arrival in Annapolis of Belle Meade and her mother, who stopped at the Maryland House. Dave saw them on the only days when it was possible—-that is to say, on Saturdays and Sundays. He had many glimpses of his sweetheart, however, at other times, for Belle, filled with the fascination of Naval life, came often with her mother to watch the outdoor drills.

When Dave saw her at such times, however, he was obliged to act as though he did not. Not by look or sign could he convey any intimation that he was doing anything but pay the strictest heed to duty.

Then came the Saturday before examination. Dave Darrin, released after dinner, would gladly have hurried away from the Academy grounds to visit his sweetheart in town, but Belle willed it otherwise.

"These are your last days here, Dave, " whispered Belle, as she and her handsome midshipman strolled about. "If I'm to share your life with you, I may as well begin by sharing the Naval Academy with you to-day. "

"Shall we go over to the field and watch the ball game when it starts? " Darrin asked.

"Not unless you very especially wish to, " Miss Meade replied. "I'd rather have you to myself than to share your attention with a ball game. "

So, though Midshipman Dave was interested in the outcome of the game, he decided to wait for the score when it had been made.

"Where's Dan to-day? " Belle inquired.

"Over at the ball game. "

"Alone? "

"No; the brigade is with him, or he's with the brigade, " laughed Darrin.

"Then he's not there with a girl? "

"Oh, no; I think Danny's second experience has made him a bit skeptical about girls. "

"And how are you, on that point, Mr. Darrin? " teased Belle, gazing up at him mirthfully.

"You know my sentiments, as to myself, Belle. As for Dan--well, I think it beyond doubt that he will do well to wait for several years before he allows himself to be interested in any girls. "

"Why? "

"Well, because Danny's judgment is bad in that direction. And he's pretty sure to be beaten out by any determined rival. You see, when Danny gets interested in a girl, he doesn't really know whether he wants her. From a girl's point of view what do you think of that failing, Belle? "

"I am afraid the girl is not likely to feel complimented. "

"So, " pursued Dave, "while Danny is really interested in a girl, but is uneasily unable to make up his mind, the girl is pretty sure to grow tired of him and take up with the more positive rival. "

"Poor Dan is not likely to have a bride early in life, " sighed Belle.

"Oh, yes; one very excellent bride for a Naval officer to have. "

"What is that? "

"His commission. Dan, if he keeps away from too interesting girls, will have some years in which to fit himself splendidly in his profession. By that time he'll be all the better equipped for taking care of a wife. "

"I wonder, " pondered Belle, "what kind of wife Dan will finally choose. "

"He won't have anything to do with the choosing, " laughed Darrin. "One of these days some woman will choose him, and then Dan will be anchored for life. It is even very likely that he'll imagine that he selected his wife from among womankind, but he won't have much to say about it. "

"You seem to think Dan is only half witted, " Belle remarked.

"Only where women are concerned, Belle. In everything else he's a most capable young American. He's going to be a fine Naval officer. "

In another hour Belle had changed her mind. She had seen all of the Academy grounds that she cared about for a while, and now proposed that they slip out through the Maryland Avenue gate for a walk through the shaded, sweet scented streets of Annapolis. As Darrin had town liberty the plan pleased him.

Strolling slowly the young people at last neared State Circle.

"I thought midshipmen didn't tell fibs, " suddenly remarked Belle.

"They're not supposed to, " Dave replied.

"But you said Dan was at the ball game. "

"Isn't he? "

"Look there! " Belle exclaimed dramatically.

CHAPTER XX

DAN STEERS ON THE ROCKS AGAIN

Just entering Wiegard's were Midshipman Dalzell and a very pretty young woman.

Dan had not caught sight of his approaching friends.

"Why, that fellow told me he was going to see if he couldn't be the mascot for a winning score to-day, " Dave exclaimed.

"But he didn't say that the score was to be won in a ball game, did he? " Belle queried demurely.

"Now I think of it, he didn't mention ball, " Darrin admitted. "But I thought it was the game down on the Academy athletic field. "

"No; it was very different kind of game, " Belle smiled. "Dave, you'll find that Dan is incurable. He's going to keep on trying with women until— —-"

"Until he lands one? " questioned Dave.

"No; until one lands him. Dave, I wonder if it would be too terribly prying if we were to turn into Wiegard's too? "

"I don't see any reason why it should be, " Darrin answered. "Mr. Wiegard conducts a public confectioner's place. It's the approved place for any midshipman to take a young lady for ice cream. Do you feel that you'd like some ice cream? "

"No, " Belle replied honestly. "But I'd like to get a closer look at Dan's latest. "

So Dave led his sweetheart into Wiegard's. In order to get a seat at a table it was necessary to pass the table at which Dan and his handsome friend were seated. As Dalzell's back was toward the door he did not espy his friends until they were about to pass.

"Why, hello, Darry! " cried Dan, rising eagerly, though his cheeks flushed a bit. "How do you do, Miss Meade? Miss Henshaw, may I present my friends? Miss Meade and Mr. Darrin. "

The introduction was pleasantly acknowledged all around. Miss Henshaw proved wholly well-bred and at ease.

"Won't you join us here? " asked Dalzell, trying hard to conceal the fact that he didn't want any third and fourth parties.

"I know you'll excuse us, " answered Dave, bowing, "and I feel certain that I am running counter to Miss Meade's wishes. But I have so little opportunity to talk to her that I'm going to beg you to excuse us. I'm going to be selfish and entice Miss Meade away to the furthest corner. "

That other table was so far away that Dave and Belle could converse in low tones without the least danger of being overheard. There were, at that time, no other patrons in the place.

"Well, Belle, what do you think of the lady, now that you've seen her? "

"You've named her, " replied Belle quietly. "Dan's new friend is beyond any doubt a lady. "

"Then Dan is safe, at last. "

"I'm not so sure of that, " Belle answered.

"But, if she's really a lady, she must be safe company for Dan. "

Belle smiled queerly before she responded:

"I'm afraid Dan is in for a tremendous disappointment. "

"In the lady's character? " pressed Darrin.

"Oh, indeed, no. "

"Wait and see. "

"But I'd rather know now. "

"I'll tell you what I mean before you say good-bye this afternoon, " Belle promised.

"By Jove, but I am afraid that is going to be too late, " murmured Midshipman Darrin. "Unless I'm greatly misled as to the meaning of the light that has suddenly come into Danny's eyes, he's proposing to her now! "

"Oh! " gasped Belle, and the small spoonful of cream that was passing down her throat threatened to strangle her.

"Dave, how old do you think Miss Henshaw is? " asked Miss Meade, as soon as she could trust herself to speak.

"Twenty, I suppose. "

"You don't know much about women's ages, then, do you? " smiled Belle.

"I don't suppose I've any business to know. "

"Miss Henshaw is a good many years older than Dan. "

"She doesn't look it, " urged Dave.

"But she is. Trust another woman to know! "

"There, by Jove! " whispered Dave. "It has started. Danny is running under the wire! I can tell by his face that he has just started to propose. "

"Poor boy! He'll have an awful fall! " muttered Belle.

"Why do you say that? But, say! You're right, Belle. Dan's face has turned positively ghastly. He looks worse than he could if he'd just failed to graduate. "

"Naturally, " murmured Belle. "Poor boy, I'm sorry for him. "

"But what's the matter? "

"Did you notice Miss Henshaw's jewelry? "

"Not particularly. I can see, from here, that she's wearing a small diamond in each ear. "

"Dave, didn't you see the flat gold band that she wears on the third finger of her left hand? " Belle demanded in a whisper.

"No, " confessed Midshipman Darrin innocently. "But what has that to do with—-"

"Her wedding ring, " Belle broke in. "Dan has gotten her title twisted. She's Mrs. Henshaw. "

"Whew! But what, in that case, is she doing strolling around with a midshipman? That's no proper business for a married woman, " protested Dave Darrin.

"Haven't you called on or escorted any married women since you've been at Annapolis? " demanded Belle bluntly.

"Yes; certainly, " nodded Dave. "But, in every instance they were wives of Naval officers, and such women looked upon midshipmen as mere little boys. "

"Isn't there an Admiral Henshaw in the Navy? " inquired Belle.

"Certainly. "

"That's Mrs. Henshaw, " Belle continued.

"How do you know? "

"I don't, but I'm certain, just the same. Now, Dan has met Mrs. Henshaw somewhere down at the Naval Academy. He heard her name and got it twisted into Miss Henshaw. It's his own blundering fault, no doubt. But Admiral Henshaw's young and pretty wife is not to be blamed for allowing a boyish midshipman to stroll with her as her escort. "

"Whew! " whistled Dave Darrin under his breath. "So Dan has been running it blind again? Oh, Belle, it's a shame! I'm heartily sorry that we've been here to witness the poor old chap's Waterloo. "

"So am I, " admitted Belle. "But the harm that has been done is due to Dan's own blindness. He should learn to read ordinary signs as he runs. "

No wonder Dan Dalzell's face had gone gray and ashy. For the time being he was feeling keenly. He had been so sure of "Miss" Henshaw's being a splendid woman—-as, indeed, she was—-that he decided on this, their third meeting, to try his luck with a sailor's impetuous wooing. In other words, he had plumply asked the admiral's wife to marry him;

"Why, you silly boy! " remonstrated Mrs. Henshaw, glancing up at him with a dismayed look. "I don't know your exact age, Mr. Dalzell, but I think it probable that I am at least ten years older than—-"

"I don't care, " Dan maintained bravely.

"Besides, what would the admiral say? "

"Is he your father or your brother? " Dan inquired.

"My husband! "

Then it was that Midshipman Dalzell's face had gone so suddenly gray. He fairly gasped and felt as though he were choking.

"Mr. Dalzell, " spoke Mrs. Henshaw, earnestly, "let us both forget that you ever spoke such unfortunate words. Let us forget it all, and let it pass as though nothing had happened at all. I will confess that, two or three times, I thought you addressed me as 'miss. ' I believed it to be only a slip of the tongue. I didn't dream that you didn't know. Even if I were a single woman I wouldn't think of encouraging you for a moment, for I am much—-much—-too old for you. And now, let us immediately forget it all, Mr. Dalzell. Shall we continue our stroll? "

Somehow the dazed midshipman managed to reply gracefully, and to follow his fair companion from Wiegard's.

"Poor Dan! " sighed Dave. "I'll wager that's the worst crusher that Dalzell ever had. But how do you read so much at a glance, Belle? "

"By keeping my eyes moderately well opened, " that young woman answered simply.

"I wonder where poor Dan's adventures in search of a wife are going to end up? " mused Darrin.

"He'd better accept the course that you outlined for him a little while ago, " half smiled Belle. "Dan's very best course will be to devote his thoughts wholly to his profession for a few years, and wait until the right woman comes along and chooses him for herself. You may tell Dan, from me, some time, if it won't hurt his feelings, that I think his only safe course is to shut his eyes and let the woman do the choosing. "

"I must be a most remarkably fine fellow myself, " remarked Midshipman Darrin modestly.

"Why do you think that? "

"Why, a girl with eyes as sharp as yours, Belle, would never have accepted me if there had been a visible flaw on me anywhere. "

"There are no very pronounced flaws except those that I can remedy when I take charge of you, Dave, " replied Belle with what might have been disconcerting candor.

"Then I'm lucky in at least one thing, " laughed Darrin good-humoredly. "When my turn comes I shall be made over by a most capable young woman. Then I shall be all but flawless. "

"Or else I shall take a bride's privilege, " smiled Belle demurely, "and go back to mother. "

"You'll have plenty of time for that, " teased Dave. "A Naval officer's time is spent largely at sea, and he can't take his wife with him. "

"Don't remind me of that too often, " begged Belle, a plaintive note in her voice. "Your being at sea so much is the only flaw that I see in the future. And, as neither of us will be rich, I can't follow you around the world much of the time. "

When Midshipman Dave Darrin reentered his quarters late that afternoon be found Dan Dalzell sitting back in a chair, his hands thrust deep into his pockets. His whole attitude was one of most unmilitary dejection.

"Dave, I've run the ship aground again, " Dan confessed ruefully.

"I know you have, Danny, " Darrin replied sympathetically.

Dan Dalzell bounded to his feet.

"What? " he gasped. "Is the story going the rounds? "

"It can't be. "

"Then did you hear what we were saying this afternoon in Wiegard's? "

"No; we were too far away for that. But I judged that you had succeeded in making Mrs. Henshaw feel very uncomfortable for a few moments. "

"Then you knew she was a married woman, Dave? "

"No; but Belle did. "

"How, I—-wonder? "

"She saw the wedding ring on Mrs. Henshaw's left hand. "

Dan Dalzell looked the picture of amazement. Then he whistled in consternation.

"By the great Dewey! " he groaned hoarsely. "I never thought of that! "

"No; but you should have done so. "

"Dave, I'm the biggest chump in the world. Will you do me a supreme favor—-kick me? "

"That would be too rough, Dan. But, if you can stand it, Belle offered me some good advice for you in your affairs with women. "

"Thank her for me, when you get a chance, but I don't need it, " replied Dan bitterly. "I'm through with trying to find a sweetheart, or any candidate to become Mrs. Dalzell. "

"But you'd better listen to the advice, " Dave insisted, and repeated what Belle had said.

"By Jove, Dave, but you're lucky to be engaged to a sensible girl like Belle! I wish there was another like her in the world. "

"Why? "

"If there were another like Belle I'd be sorely tempted to try my \ luck for the fourth time. "

"Dan Dalzell! " cried Dave sternly. "You're not safe without a guardian! You'll do it again, between now and graduation. "

"You can watch me, if you want, then; but I'll fool you, " smiled Dan. "But say, Dave! "

"Well? "

"You don't suppose Belle will say anything about this back in Gridley, do you? By Jove, if she does I'd feel— — -

"You'll feel something else, " warned Dave snappily, "if you don't at once assure me that you know Belle too well to think that she'd make light of your misfortunes. "

"But sometimes girls tell one another some things— — -"

"Belle Meade doesn't, " interrupted Dave so briskly that Dalzell, after a glance, agreed:

"You're right there, David, little giant. I've known Belle ever since we were kids at the Central Grammar School. If Belle ever got into any trouble through too free use of her tongue, then I never heard anything about it. "

"Dan, do you want a fine suggestion about the employment of the rest of your liberty time while we're at Annapolis? "

"Yes. "

"You remember Barnes's General History, that we used to have in Grammar school? "

"Yes. "

"Devote your liberty time to reading the book through again. "

CHAPTER XXI

IN THE THICK OF DISASTER

Examination week—-torture of the "wooden" and seventh heaven of the "savvy! "

For the wooden man, he who knows little, this week of final examinations is a period of unalloyed torture. He must go before an array of professors who are there to expose his ignorance.

No "wooden" man can expect to get by. The gates of hope are closed before his face. He marches to the ordeal, full of a dull misery. Whether he is fourth classman or first, he knows that hope has fled; that he will go below the saving 2.5 mark and be dropped from the rolls.

But your "savvy" midshipman—-he who knows much, and who is sure and confident with his knowledge, finds this week of final examinations a period of bliss and pride. He is going to "pass"; he knows that, and nothing else matters.

Eight o'clock every morning, during this week, finds the midshipman in one recitation room or another, undergoing his final. As it is not the purpose of the examiners to wear any man out, the afternoon is given over to pleasures. There are no afternoon examinations, and no work of any sort that can be avoided. Indeed, the "savvy" man has a week of most delightful afternoons, with teas, lawn parties, strolls both within and without the walls of the Academy grounds, and many boating parties. It is in examination week that the young ladies flock to Annapolis in greater numbers than ever.

Sometimes the "wooden" midshipman, knowing there is no further hope for him, rushes madly into the pleasures of this week, determined to carry back into civil life with him the memories of as many Annapolis pleasures as possible.

A strong smattering there is of midshipmen who, by no means "savvy, " are yet not so "wooden" but that they hope, by hard study at the last to pull through on a saving margin in marks.

These desperate ones do not take part in the afternoon pleasures, for these midshipmen, with furrowed brows, straining eyes, feverish skin and dogged determination, spend their afternoons and evenings in one final assault on their text-books in the hope of pulling through.

Dave Darrin was not one of the honor men of his class, but he was "savvy" just the same. Dan Dalzell was a few notches lower in the class standing, but Dan was as sure of graduation as was his chum.

"One thing goes for me, this week, " announced Dan, just before the chums hustled out to dinner formation on Monday.

"What's that? " Dave wanted to know. "No girls; no tender promenades! " grumbled Midshipman Dalzell.

"Poor old chap, " muttered Dave sympathetically.

"Oh, that's all right for you, " grunted Dan. "You have one of the 'only' girls, and so you're safe. "

"There are more 'only' girls than you've any idea of, Dan Dalzell, " Dave retorted with spirit. "The average American girl is a mighty fine, sweet, wholesome proposition. "

"I'll grant that, " nodded Dan, with a knowing air. "But I've made an important discovery concerning the really fine girls. "

"Produce the discovery, " begged Darrin. "The really fine girl, " announced Dan, in a hollow voice, "prefers some other fellow to me. "

"Well, I guess that'll be a fine idea for you to nurse—-until after graduation, " reflected Darrin aloud. "I'm not going to seek to undeceive you, Danny boy. "

So Dave went off to meet Belle and her mother, while Dan Dalzell hunted up another first classman who also believed that the girls didn't particularly esteem him. That other fellow was Midshipman Jetson.

"Mrs. Davis is giving a lawn party this afternoon, " announced Dave, after he had lifted his cap in greeting of Mrs. Meade and her daughter. "I have an invitation from Mrs. Davis to escort you both over to her house. Of course, if you find the tea and chatter a bit dull over there, we can go somewhere else presently. "

"I never find anything dull that is a part of the life here, " returned Belle, little enthusiast for the Navy. "It will suit you, mother? "

"Anything at all will suit me, " declared Mrs. Meade amiably. "David, just find me some place where I can drop into an armchair and have some other middle-aged woman like myself to talk with. Then you young people need pay no further heed to me. Examination week doesn't last forever. "

"It doesn't, " laughed Darrin, "and many of our fellows are very thankful for that. "

"How are you going to come through? " Belle asked, with a quick little thrill of anxiety.

"Nothing to worry about on that score, " Dave assured her. "I'm sufficiently 'savvy' to pull sat. all right. "

"Isn't that fine? And Dan? "

"Oh, he'll finish sat., too, if he doesn't sight another craft flying pink hair ribbons. "

"Any danger of that? " asked Belle anxiously, for Dan was a townsman of hers.

"Not judging by the company that Dan is keeping to-day, " smiled Darrin.

"Who is his companion to-day, then? "

"Jetson, a woman hater. "

"Really a woman hater? " asked Belle.

"Oh, no; Jet wouldn't poison all girls, or do anything like that. He isn't violent against girls. In fact, he's merely shy when they're around. But in the service any fellow who isn't always dancing attendance on the fair is doomed to be dubbed a woman hater. In other words, a woman hater is just a fellow who doesn't pester girls all the time. "

"Are you a woman hater? " Belle asked.

"Except when you are at Annapolis, " was Dave's ready explanation.

That afternoon's lawn party proved a much more enjoyable affair than the young people had expected. Belle met there, for the first time, five or six girls with whom she was to be thrown often later on.

When it was over, Dave, having town liberty as well, proudly escorted his sweetheart and her mother back to the hotel.

There were more days like it. Dave, by Thursday, realizing that he was coming through his morning trials with flying colors, had arranged permission to take out a party in one of the steamers.

As the steamer could be used only for a party Darrin invited Farley and Wolgast to bring their sweethearts along. Mrs. Meade at first demurred about going.

"You and Belle have had very little time together, " declared that good lady, "and I'm not so old but that I remember my youth. With so large a party there's no need of a chaperon. "

"But we'd immensely like to have you come, " urged Dave; "that is, unless you'd be uncomfortable on the water. "

"Oh, I'm never uncomfortable on the water, " Belle's mother replied.

"Then you'll come, won't you? " pleaded Dave. Belle's mother made one of the jolly party.

"You'd better come, too, Danny boy, " urged Dave at the last moment. "There'll be no unattached girl with the party, so you'll be vastly safer with us than you would away from my watchful eye. "

"Huh! A fine lot your watchful eye has been on me this week, " retorted Midshipman Dalzell. "Jetson has been my grandmother this week. "

It was a jolly party that steamed down Chesapeake Bay in the launch that afternoon. There was an enlisted man of the engineer department at the engine, while a seaman acted as helmsman.

"Straight down the bay, helmsman, " Dave directed, as the launch headed out.

"Aye, aye, sir, " replied the man, touching his cap.

After that the young people—-Mrs. Meade was included under that heading—-gave themselves over to enjoyment. Belle, with a quiet twinkle in her eyes that was born of the love of teasing, tried very hard to draw Mr. Jetson out, thereby causing that young man to flush many times.

Dan, from the outset, played devoted squire to Mrs. Meade. That was safe ground for him.

"What's that party in the sailboat yonder? " inquired Mrs. Meade, when the steamer had been nearly an hour out. "Are the young men midshipman or officers? "

Dave raised to his eyes the glasses with which the steamer was equipped.

"They're midshipmen, " he announced. "Gray and Lambert, of our class, and Haynes and Whipple of the second class. "

"They've young ladies with them. "

"Certainly. "

"Isn't it rather risky for midshipmen to have control of the boat, then, with no older man along? " asked Mrs. Meade.

"It ought not to be, " Dave replied. "Midshipmen of the upper classes are expected to be familiar with the handling of sailboats. "

"Those fellows are getting careless, at any rate, " muttered Dan Dalzell. "Look at the way that sail is behaving. Those fellows are paying too much attention to the girls and too little heed to the handling of the craft! "

Even as Dalzell spoke the helm was jammed over and the boat started to come about.

"Confound Lambert! He ought to ease off his sheet a good bit, " snapped Midshipman Dalzell.

"Helmsman, point our boat so as to pass under the other craft's stern, " spoke Darrin so quietly that only Dan and Belle overheard him.

"Aye, aye, sir, " murmured the helmsman, in a very low voice. Dave signaled the engineman silently to increase the speed.

"There the boat goes, the sail caught by a cross current of air! " called Midshipman Dalzell almost furiously.

The girls aboard the sailboat now cried out in alarm as they felt the extreme list of the boat under them. All too late Midshipman Gray Sprang for the sheet to ease it off.

Too late! In another moment the sailboat had capsized, the mast nearly snapping in the blow over.

"Make haste—-do! " cried Mrs. Meade, rising in the steamer.

But the steamer was already under increased headway, and the helmsman had to make but a slight turn to bear down directly to the scene of the disaster.

Three midshipmen could be seen floundering in the water, each steadily supporting the head of a girl. But the fourth, midshipman was floundering about wildly. Then he disappeared beneath the water.

"That young man has given up and gone down! " cried Mrs. Meade, whom Dave had just persuaded to resume her seat.

"No, " Dave assured her. "Gray isn't drowning. But his girl companion is missing, and he has dived to find her. "

"Then the girl is lost! " quivered Mrs. Meade.

"No; I think not. Gray is a fine swimmer, and will find Miss Butler before she has been under too long a time. "

Then Dave rose, for he was commander here. "Danny boy, throw off your shoes and blouse and cap. The rest stand by the boat to give such aid as you can. Ladies, you'll excuse us. "

Thereupon Dave Darrin doffed his own cap, blouse and shoes. He and Dalzell were the two best swimmers in the party, and it looked as though there would be work ahead for them to do.

In another moment the steamer was on the scene, and speed was shut off. Lambert, Haynes and Whipple, with their girl companions, were speedily reached and hauled aboard.

Then Gray came up, but alone.

"Hasn't Pauline come up? " he gasped in terror.

"No, " Darrin replied shortly, but in a voice laden with sympathy.

"Then I've got to down again, " replied Gray despairingly. "I'd better stay down, too. "

He sank instantly, a row of bubbles coming up at the spot where he had vanished.

"The poor, unfortunate fellow! He won't really attempt to drown himself, will he, if he doesn't find his young woman friend? " inquired Mrs. Meade.

"No, " Dave answered without turning. "And we wouldn't allow him to do so, either. "

Dave waited but a brief interval, this time. Then, as Midshipman Gray did not reappear, he called:

"Danby! "

"Yes, sir, " replied the enlisted man by the engine.

"Hustle forward and rig a rope loop to the anchor cable. How long is the anchor? "

"About three feet, sir. "

"Then rig the loop two feet above the mudhook. "

"Yes, sir. "

"Hustle! "

"Yes, sir. "

"Is Gray trying to stay under? Trying to drown himself as a sign of his repentance? " whispered Wolgast in Dave's ear. But Darrin shook his head. An instant later Gray shot up to the surface—-alone!

"Come aboard, " ordered Dave Darrin, but he did not rely entirely on coaxing. Snatching up a boat-hook he fastened it in Gray's collar and drew that midshipman alongside, where many ready hands stretched out and hauled him aboard.

Two of the rescued young women were now sobbing almost hysterically.

"If you won't let me stay in the water, won't some of the rest of you do something? " demanded Midshipman Gray hoarsely.

"We're going to, " nodded Dave. "Danby! "

"Yes, sir. "

"Let go the anchor. "

"Very good, sir. "

"Follow me, Dan, " directed Dave. The anchor went overboard while the two midshipmen were hustling forward.

"I'm going down first, Danny, " explained Dave. "Follow whenever you may think you need to, but don't be in too big a hurry. Use good judgment. "

"Trust me, " nodded Dan hoarsely.

With that Dave seized the visible part of the anchor cable and went down, forcing himself toward the bottom by holding to the cable. It was a difficult undertaking, as, after he had gone part of the way, the buoyancy of the water fought against his efforts to go lower. But Midshipman Darrin still gripped hard at the cable, fighting foot by foot. His eyes open, at last he sighted the loop near the anchor. With a powerful effort he reached that loop, thrusting his left arm through it. The strain almost threatened to break that arm, but Dave held grimly, desperately on.

Now he looked about him. Fortunately there was no growth of seaweed at this point, and he could see clearly for a distance of quite a few yards around him.

"Queer what can have become of the body! " thought Darrin. "But then, the boat has drifted along slightly, and Miss Butler may have sunk straight down. She may be lying or floating here just out of my range of vision. I wish I could let go and strike out, but I'd only shoot up to the surface after a little. "

Many a shadow in the deep water caused Darrin to start and peer the harder, only to find that he had been deceived.

At that depth the weight of the water pressed dangerously upon his head and in his ears. Dave felt his senses leaving him.

"I'd sooner die than give up easily! " groaned the young midshipman, and he seemed about to have his wish.

CHAPTER XXII

THE SEARCH AT THE BOTTOM OF THE BAY

By the strongest effort of the will that he could make, Darrin steadied himself and forced his eyes once more open.

Drifting toward him, two feet above his head, was what looked like another shadow. It came closer.

At the first thought Darrin was inclined not to believe his senses.

"I'll have to go up, after all, and let Dan have his chance. I'm seeing things, " Dave decided.

For, though the object floating toward him had some of the semblance of a skirt-clad figure, yet it looked all out of proportion--perhaps twice the size of Pauline Butler.

That was a trick of the scanty light coming through the water at an angle--this coupled with Darrin's own fatigue of the eyes.

Closer it came, and looked a bit smaller.

"It is a girl--a woman--some human being! " throbbed Dave internally.

Now, though his head seeming bursting, Dave hung on more tightly than ever. The drift of the water was bringing the body slowly nearer to him. He must hold on until he could let himself strike upward, seizing that body in his progress.

At last the moment arrived. Dave felt a hard tug at the cable, but he did not at that instant realize that Dan Dalzell had just started down from the steamer.

Dave judged that the right instant had come. He let go of the loop, and was shot upward. But, as he moved, his spread arms caught hold of the floating figure.

Up to within a few feet of the surface Darrin and his burden moved easily. Then he found it necessary to kick out hard with his feet.

Thus he carried the burden clear, to the open air above, though at a distance of some forty feet from the steamer.

"There they are! " Farley's voice was heard calling, and there was a splash.

"Bully for you, old fellow! Hold her up, and I'm with you! " hailed Midshipman Farley.

In another moment Dave Darrin had been eased of his human burden, and Farley was swimming to the steamer with the senseless form of Pauline Butler.

Darrin tried to swim, and was astounded at finding himself so weak in the water. He floated, propelling himself feebly with his hands, completely exhausted.

Just at that moment nearly every eye was fixed on Farley and his motionless burden, and many pairs of hands stretched out to receive them.

Yet the gaze of one alert pair of eyes was fixed on Darrin, out there beyond.

"Now, you'd better look after Dave, " broke in the quiet, clear voice of Belle Meade. "I think he needs help. "

Wolgast went over the side in an instant, grappling with Midshipman Darrin and towing him to the side of the boat.

"All in! " cried Midshipman Gray jubilantly.

"Except Dan. Where's he? " muttered Dave weakly, as he sat on one of the side seats.

"I'll signal him, " muttered Wolgast, and hastened forward to the anchor cable. This he seized and shook clumsily several times. The vibrated motion must have been imparted downward, for soon Dan Dalzell's head came above water.

"Everyone all right? " called Dan, as soon as he had gulped in a mouthful of air.

"O. K." nodded Wolgast. "Come alongside and let me haul you in. "

"You let me alone, " muttered Dalzell, coming alongside and grasping the rail. "Do you think a short cold bath makes me too weak to attend to myself? "

With that Dan drew himself aboard. Back in the cockpit Mrs. Meade and some of the girls were in frenzied way doing their best to revive Pauline Butler, who, at the present moment, showed no signs of life.

"Let me take charge of this reviving job. I've taken several tin medals in first aid to the injured, " proclaimed Farley modestly.

In truth the midshipman had a decided knack for this sort of work. He assailed it with vigor, making a heap of life preservers, and over these placing Miss Butler, head downward. Then Farley took vigorous charge of the work of "rolling" out the water that Miss Butler must have taken into her system.

"Get anchor up and start the steamer back to Annapolis at the best speed possible, " ordered Dave, long before he could talk in a natural voice.

Wolgast and Dan aided Danny in hoisting the anchor. Steam was crowded on and the little craft cut a swift, straight path for Annapolis.

"Pauline is opening her eyes! " cried Farley, after twenty minutes more of vigorous work in trying to restore the girl.

The girl's eyes merely fluttered, though, as a slight sigh escaped her. The eyelids fell again, and there was but a trace of motion at the pulse.

"We mustn't lose the poor child, now that we've succeeded in proving a little life there, " cried Mrs. Meade anxiously.

"Now, that's what I call a reflection on the skill of Dr. Farley, " protested that midshipman in mock indignation. It was necessary, at any amount of trouble, to keep these women folks on fair spirits until Annapolis was reached. Then, perhaps, many of them would faint.

All of the dry jackets of midshipmen aboard had been thrown protectingly around the girls who had been in the water.

"Torpedo boat ahead, sir, " reported the helmsman.

"Give her the distress signal to lie to, " directed Dave.

The engine's whistle sent out the shrieking appeal over the waters. The destroyer was seen to heave about and come slowly to meet the steamer.

Long before the two craft had come together Dave Darrin was standing, holding to one of the awning stanchions, for he was not yet any too strong.

"Destroyer, ahoy! " he shouted as loudly as he could between his hands. "Have you a surgeon aboard? "

"Yes, " came back the answer.

"Let us board you, sir! "

"What's— —-"

But Dave had turned to the helmsman with:

"Steam up alongside. Lose no time. "

In a very short space of time the destroyer was reached and the steamer ran alongside. The unconscious form of Miss Butler was passed up over the side, followed by the other members of the sailboat party. Mrs. Meade followed, in case she could be of any assistance.

"You may chaperon your party of young ladies in the steamer, Belle, " smiled Mrs. Meade from the deck of the destroyer. "I give you express authority over them. "

Farley's and Wolgast's sweethearts laughed merrily at this. All hands had again reached the point where laughter came again to their lips without strong effort. Pauline Butler was safe under the surgeon's hands, if anywhere.

Then the destroyers pulled out again, hitting a fast clip for Annapolis.

"That's the original express boat; this is only a cattle-carrier, " muttered Dave, gazing after the fast destroyer.

"Calling us cattle, are you? " demanded Belle. "As official chaperon I must protest on behalf of the young ladies aboard. "

"A cattle boat often carries human passengers, " Dave returned. "I call this a cattle boat only because of our speed. "

"We don't need speed now, " Belle answered. "Those who do are on board the destroyer. "

By the time that the steamer reached her berth at the Academy wall, and the young people had hastened ashore, they learned that Pauline Butler had been removed to a hospital in Annapolis; that she was very much alive, though still weak, and that in a day or two she would again be all right.

With a boatswain's mate in charge, another steamer was despatched down the bay to recover and tow home the capsized sailboat.

Examination week went through to its finish. By Saturday night the first classmen knew who had passed. But two of the members of the class had "bilged. " Dave, Dan and all their close friends in the class had passed and had no ordeal left at Annapolis save to go through the display work of Graduation Week.

"You still have your two years at sea, though, before you're sure of your commission, " sighed Belle, as they rested between dances that Saturday night.

"Any fellow who can live through four years at Annapolis can get through the two years at sea and get his commission at last, " laughed Dave Darrin happily. "Have no fears, Belle, about my being an ensign, if I have the good fortune to live two years more. "

CHAPTER XXIII

GRADUATION DAY--AT LAST

Graduation Week!

Now came the time when the Naval Academy was given over to the annual display of what could be accomplished in the training of midshipmen.

There were drills and parades galore, with sham battles in which the sharp crack of rifle fire was punctured by the louder, steadier booms of field artillery. There were gun-pointing contests aboard the monitors and other practice craft.

There were exhibitions of expert boat-handling, and less picturesque performances at the machine shops and in the engine and dynamo rooms. There were other drills and exhibitions--enough of them to weary the reader, as they doubtless did weary the venerable members of a Board of Visitors appointed by the President.

On Wednesday night came the class german. Now our young first classmen were in for another thrill--the pleasure of wearing officers' uniforms for the first time.

On graduation the midshipman is an officer of the Navy, though a very humble one. The graduated midshipman's uniform is a more imposing affair than the uniform of a midshipman who is still merely a member of the brigade at the Naval Academy.

On this Wednesday evening the new uniforms were of white, the summer and tropical uniform of the Navy. These were donned by first classmen only in honor of the class german, which the members of the three lower classes do not attend.

All the young Women attending were also attired wholly in white, save for simple jewelry or coquettish ribbons.

Dave Darrin, of course, escorted Belle Meade with all the pride in the world. Most of the other midshipmen "dragged" young women on this great evening.

Dan Dalzell did not. He attended merely for the purpose of looking on, save when he danced with Belle Meade.

On the following evening, after another tiresome day spent in boring the Board of Visitors, came the evening promenade, a solemnly joyous and very dressy affair.

Then came that memorable graduation morning, when so many dozens of young midshipmen, since famous in the Navy, received their diplomas.

Early the young men turned out.

"It seems queer to be turning out without arms, doesn't it? " grumbled Dan Dalzell.

But it is the rule for the graduating class to turn out without arms on this one very grand morning. The band formed on the right of line. Next to them marched to place the graduating class, minus arms. Then the balance of the brigade under arms.

When the word was given a drum or two sounded the step, and off the brigade marched, slowly and solemnly. A cornet signal, followed by a drum roll, and then the Naval Academy Band crashed into the joyous march, consecrated to this occasion, "Ain't I glad I'm out of the wilderness! "

"Amen! Indeed I'm glad, " Dave Darrin murmured devoutly under his breath. "There has been many a time in the last four years when I didn't expect to graduate. But now it's over. Nothing can stop Dan or myself! "

Crowds surrounded the entrance to the handsome, classic chapel, though the more favored crowds had already passed inside and filled the seats that are set apart for spectators.

Inside filed the midshipmen, going to their seats in front. The chaplain, in the hush that followed the seating, rose, came forward and in a voice husky with emotion urged:

"Friends, let us pray for the honor, success, glory and steadfast manhood through life of the young men who are about to go forth with their diplomas. "

Every head was bowed while the chaplain's petition ascended.

When the prayer was over the superintendent, in full dress uniform, stepped to the front of the rostrum and made a brief address. Sailors are seldom long-winded talkers. The superintendent's address, on this very formal occasion, lasted barely four minutes. But what he said was full of earnest manhood and honest patriotism.

Then the superintendent dropped to his chair. There were not so very many dry eyes when the choir beautifully intoned:

"God be with you till we meet again! "

But now another figure appeared on the rostrum. Though few of the young men had ever seen this new-comer, they knew him by instinct. At a signal from an officer standing at the side of the chapel, the members of the brigade broke forth into thunderous hurrahs. For this man, now about to address them, was their direct chief.

"Gentlemen and friends, " announced the superintendent, "I take the greatest pleasure that may come to any of us in introducing our chief—-the Secretary of the Navy. "

And now other officers appeared on the rostrum, bearing diplomas and arranging them in order.

The name of the man to graduate first in his class was called. He went forward and received his diploma from the Secretary, who said:

"Mr. Ennerly, it is, indeed, a high honor to take first place in such a class as yours! "

Ennerly, flushed and proud, returned to his seat amid applause from his comrades.

And so there was a pleasant word for each midshipman as he went forward.

When the Secretary picked up the seventeenth diploma he called:

"David Darrin! "

Who was the most popular man in the brigade of midshipmen? The midshipmen themselves now endeavored to answer the question by the tremendous explosions of applause with which they embarrassed Dave as he went forward.

"Mr. Darrin, " smiled the Secretary, "there are no words of mine that can surpass the testimonial which you have just received from your comrades. But I will add that we expect tremendous things from you, sir, within the next few years. You have many fine deeds and achievements to your credit here, sir. Within the week you led in a truly gallant rescue human life down the bay. Mr. Darrin, in handing you your well-earned diploma, I take upon myself the liberty of congratulating your parents on their son! "

As Dave returned to his seat with his precious sheepskin the elder Darrin, who was in the audience, took advantage of the renewed noises of applause to clear his throat huskily several times. Dave's mother honestly used her handkerchief to dry the tears of pride that were in her eyes.

Another especial burst of applause started when Daniel Dalzell, twenty-first in his class, was called upon to go forward.

"I didn't believe Danny Grin would ever get through, " one first classman confided behind his hand to another. "I expected that the upper classmen would kill Danny Grin before he ever got over being a fourth classman. "

But here was Dan coming back amid more applause, his graduation number high enough to make it practically certain that he would be a rear admiral one of these days when he had passed the middle stage of life in the service.

One by one the other diplomas were given out, each accompanied by some kindly message from the Secretary of the Navy, which, if remembered and observed, would be of great value to the graduate at some time in the future.

The graduating exercises did not last long. To devote too much time to them would be to increase the tension.

Later in the day the graduated midshipmen again appeared. They were wearing their new coats now, several inches longer in the tail, and denoting them as real officers in the Navy. A non-graduate midshipman must salute one of these graduates whenever they meet.

In their room, to be occupied but one night more, Dave and Dan finished dressing in their new uniforms at the same moment.

"Shake, Danny boy! " cried Dave Darrin, holding out his hand. "How does it seem, at last, to know that you're really an officer in the Navy? "

"Great! " gulped Dalzell. "And I don't mind admitting that, during the last four years, I've had my doubts many a time that this great day would ever come for we. But get your cap's and let's hustle outside. "

"Why this unseemly rush, Danny? "

"I want to round up a lot of under classmen and make them tire their arms out saluting me. "

"Your own arm will ache, too, then, Danny. You are obliged, as of course you know, to return every salute. "

"Hang it, yes! There's a pebble in every pickle dish, isn't there? "

"You're going to the graduation ball tonight, of course? "

"Oh, surely, " nodded Dalzell. "After working as I've worked for four years for the privilege, I'd be a fool to miss it. But I'll sneak away early, after I've done a friend's duty by you and Belle. No girls for me until I'm a captain in the Navy! "

The ball room was a scene of glory that night. Bright eyes shone unwontedly, and many a heart fluttered. For Belle Meade was not the only girl there who was betrothed to a midshipman. Any graduate who chose might marry as soon as he pleased, but nearly all the men of the class preferred to wait until they had put in their two years at sea and had won their commissions as ensigns.

"This must be a night of unalloyed pleasure to you, " murmured Belle, as she and her young officer sweetheart sat out one dance. "You can look back over a grand four years of life here. "

"I don't know that I'd have the nerve to go through it all again, " Darrin answered her honestly.

"You don't have to, " Belle laughed happily. "You put in your later boyhood here, and now your whole life of manhood is open before you. "

"I'll make the best use of that manhood that is possible for me, " Dave replied solemnly.

"You must have formed some wonderful friendships here. "

"I have. "

"And, I suppose, " hesitated Belle, "a few unavoidable enmities. "

"I don't know about that, " Dave replied promptly and with energy. "I can't think of a fellow here that I wouldn't be ready and glad to shake hands with. I hope—-I trust—-that all of the fellows in the brigade feel the same way about me. "

CHAPTER XXIV

CONCLUSION

There was one more formation yet—-one more meal to be eaten under good old Bancroft Hall.

But right after breakfast the graduates, each one now in brand-new cit. attire, began to depart in droves.

Some went to the earliest train; others stopped at the hotels and boarding houses in town to pick up relatives and friends with whom the gladsome home journey was to be made.

"I don't like you as well in cits., " declared Belle, surveying Dave critically in the hotel parlor.

"In the years to come, " smiled Dave, "you'll see quite enough of me in uniform. "

"I don't know about that, " Belle declared, her honest soul shining in her eyes. "Do you feel that you'll ever see enough of me? "

"I know that I won't, " Dave rejoined. "You have one great relief in prospect, " smiled Belle. "Whenever you do grow tired of me you can seek orders to some ship on the other side of the world. "

"The fact that I can't be at home regularly, " answered Midshipman Darrin, "is going to be the one cloud on our happiness. Never fear my seeking orders that take me from home—-unless in war time. Then, of course, every Naval officer must burn the wires with messages begging for a fighting appointment. "

"I'm not afraid of your fighting record, if the need ever comes, " replied Belle proudly. "And, Dave, though my heart breaks, I'll never show you a tear in my eyes if you're starting on a fighting cruise. "

Mrs. Meade and Dave's parents now entered the room, and soon after Danny Grin, who had gone in search of his own father and mother, returned with them.

"What are we going to do now? " asked Mr. Darrin. "I understand that we have hours to wait for the next train. "

"We can't do much, sir, " replied Dave. "Within another hour this will be the deadest town in the United States. "

"I should think you young men would want to spend most of the intervening time down at the Naval Academy, looking over the familiar spots once more, " suggested Mrs. Dalzell.

"Then I'm afraid, mother, that you don't realize much of the way that a midshipman feels. The Naval Academy is our alma mater, and a beloved spot. Yet, after what I've been through there during the last few years I don't want to see the Naval Academy again. At least, not until I've won a solid step or two in the way of promotion. "

"That's the feeling of all the graduates, I reckon, " nodded Dave Darrin. "For one, I know I don't want to go back there to-day. "

"Some day you will go back there, though, " observed Danny Grin.

"Why are you so sure? " Dave asked.

"Well, you were always such a stickler for observing the rules that the Navy Department will have to send you there for some post or other. Probably you'll go back as a discipline officer. "

"I would have one advantage over you, then, wouldn't I? " laughed Darrin. "If I had to rebuke a midshipman I could do it with a more serious face than you could. "

"I can't help my face, " sighed Danny Grin.

"You see, Dave, " Mr. Dalzell observed, with a smile, "Dan inherited his face. "

"From his father's side of the family, " promptly interposed Mrs. Dalzell.

Here Mr. Farley, also in cits., entered the parlor in his dignified fashion.

"Darry, and you, too, Danny Grin, some of the fellows are waiting outside to see you. Will you step out a moment? "

"Where are the fellows? " asked Dave unsuspectingly.

"You'll find them on the steps outside the entrance. "

Dave started for the door.

"You're wanted, too, Danny Grin, as I told you, " Farley reminded him.

"I'll be the Navy goat, then. What's the answer? " inquired Midshipman Dalzell.

"Run along, like a good little boy, and your curiosity will soon be gratified. "

Danny Grin looked as though he expected some joke, but he went none the less.

Dave, first to reach the entrance, stepped through into the open. As he did so he saw at least seventy-five of his recent classmates grouped outside.

The instant they perceived their popular comrade the crowd of graduates bellowed forth:

"N N N N,
A A A A,
V V V V,
Y Y Y Y,
NAVY!
Darrin!
Darrin!
Darrin! "

In another moment Danny Grin showed himself. Back in his face was hurled the volley:

"N N N N,
A A A A,
V V V V,

Y Y Y Y,
NAVY!
Grin!
Grin!
Grin! "

"Eh? " muttered Danny, when the last line reached him. They were unexpected. Then, as be faced the laughing eyes down in the street, Dalzell justified his nickname by one of those broad smiles that had made him famous at the Naval Academy.

Dave Darrin waved his hand in thanks for the "Four-N" yell, the surest sign of popularity, and vanished inside. When he returned to the parlor be found that Farley had conducted his parents and friends to one of the parlor windows, from which, behind drawn blinds, they had watched the scene and heard the uproar without making themselves visible.

At noon the hotel dining room was overrun with midshipmen and their friends, all awaiting the afternoon train.

But at last the time came to leave Annapolis behind in earnest. Extra cars had been put on to handle the throng, for the "train, " for the first few miles of the way, usually consists of but one combination trolley car.

"You're leaving the good old place behind, " murmured Belle, as the car started.

"Never a graduate yet but was glad to leave Annapolis behind, " replied Dave.

"It seems to me that you ought not to speak of the Naval Academy in that tone. "

"You'd understand, Belle, if you had been through every bit of the four-year grind, always with the uncertainty ahead of you of being able to get through and grad. "

"Perhaps the strict discipline irked you, too, " Miss Meade hinted.

"The strict discipline will be part of the whole professional life ahead of me, " Darrin responded. "As to discipline, it's even harder on some ships, where the old man is a stickler for having things done just so. "

"The old man? " questioned Belle.

"The 'old man' is the captain of a warship. "

"It doesn't sound respectful. "

"Yet it has always been the name given to the ship's captain, and I don't suppose it will be changed in another hundred years. How does it feel, Danny boy, going away for good? "

"Am I really going away for good? " grinned Dalzell. "I thought it was only a dream."

"Well, here's Odenton. You'll be in Baltimore after another little while, and then it will all seem more real. "

"Nothing but Gridley will look real to me on this trip, " muttered Dan. "Really, I'm growing sick for a good look at the old home town. "

"I wish you could put in the whole summer at home, Dan, " sighed his mother. "But, of course, I know that you can't. "

"No, mother; I'll have time to walk up and down the home streets two or three times, and then orders will come from the Navy Department to report aboard the ship to which I'm to be assigned. Mother, if you want to keep a boy at home you shouldn't allow him to go to a place where he's taught that nothing on earth matters but the Navy! "

Later in the afternoon the train pulled in at Baltimore. It was nearing dusk when the train pulled out of Philadelphia on its way further north.

Yet the passage of time and the speeding of country past the ear windows was barely noticed by the Gridley delegation. There was too much to talk about—-too many plans to form for the next two or three weeks of blissful leave before duty must commence again.

Here we will take leave of our young midshipmen for the present, though we shall encounter them again as they toil on upward through their careers.

We have watched Dave and Dan from their early teens. We met them first in the pages of the *"Grammar School Boys' Series. "* We know what we know of them back in the days when they attended the Central Grammar School and studied under that veteran of teachers, "Old Dut, " as he was affectionately known.

We saw them with the same chums, of Dick & Co., when that famous sextette of schoolboys entered High School. We are wholly familiar with their spirited course in the High School. We know how all six of the youngsters of Dick & Co. made the name of Gridley famous for clean and manly sports in general.

Our readers will yet hear from Dave and Dan occasionally. They appear in the pages of the *"Young Engineers' Series, "* and also in the volumes of the *"Boys of the Army Series. "*

In this latter series our young friends will learn just how the romance of Dave Darrin and Belle Meade developed; and they will also come across the similar affair of Dick Prescott and Laura Bentley.

Dave and Dan had, as they had expected, but a brief stay in the home town.

Bright and early one morning a postman handed to each a long, official envelope from the Navy Department. In each instance the envelope contained their orders to report aboard one of the Navy's biggest battleships.

Our two midshipmen were fortunate in one respect. Both were ordered to the same craft, their to finish their early Naval educations in two years of practical work as officers at sea ere they could reach the grade of ensign and step into the ward-room.

CPSIA information can be obtained
at www.ICGtesting.com
Printed in the USA
BVHW031419021120
592326BV00002B/437